DEFYING THE BILLIONAIRE'S COMMAND

DEFYING THE BILLIONAIRE'S COMMAND

BY

MICHELLE CONDER

MILLS
BOON

HarperCollins
PUBLISHERS
Since 1817

First published in Great Britain 2016
By Mills & Boon, an imprint of HarperCollins*Publishers*
1 London Bridge Street, London, SE1 9GF

Large Print edition 2017

© 2016 Michelle Conder

ISBN: 978-0-263-07048-4

Printed and bound in Great Britain
by CPI Antony Rowe, Chippenham, Wiltshire

To Mary, my mother. Thanks for being the best mother a girl could ask for.

CHAPTER ONE

IT WAS OFTEN said that Dare James was a man who had everything, and most days he'd be hard-pressed to disagree. Blessed with bad-boy good looks, and the stamina and physique any star athlete would envy, he enjoyed expensive cars, even more expensive women, and homes that spanned the globe.

A self-made billionaire by the age of thirty, he had started with nothing and now, thanks to sheer hard work and old-fashioned grit and determination, he pretty much had anything a man could want.

What he didn't have was the ability to handle fools lightly, especially pompous, fat-cat fools who understood that the stock market went up and down as long as their own wealth wasn't affected.

Dare propped his feet on his desk and leaned back in his chair. 'I don't care if he thinks we should dump the stock,' he told his CFO over the phone. 'I'm telling you to hold it. If he wants to question my judgment again he can take his business elsewhere.'

Clicking off the call, he thumbed through to the next issue he had to deal with.

'Trouble?'

Dare glanced towards his office door to find his mother framed in it. She'd flown from North Carolina to London the previous night, stopping overnight at his before she headed to Southampton to visit an old friend.

Dare smiled and dropped his feet from his desk. 'What are you doing up this early, Ma? You should still be asleep.'

His mother strolled into his office and perched on one of his sofas in the sitting area. 'I needed to talk to you before I head off today.'

Dare glanced at his watch. Business always came first in Dare's world, except when it came to his mother. 'Of course, what's up?'

If she wanted to borrow Mark, his driver, to take her to Southampton he'd already arranged it.

'I received an email from my father a month ago.'

Dare frowned, not sure he'd heard her right. 'Your father?'

'I know.' Her brow quirked. 'It was a surprise to me too.'

Dare wasn't sure what shocked him more, the fact that she'd received an email, or the fact that she'd taken so long to tell him about it. 'What does he want?'

'To see me.'

Her hands twisted together unconsciously in her lap and Dare's gut tightened. When a man who had kicked his daughter out of her home for marrying someone he didn't approve of contacted her thirty-three years later you could bet something was up. And Dare doubted it would be good.

'Bully for him,' he said without preamble.

'He invited me up to the house for lunch.'

The house being Rothmeyer House, a large stone mansion set on one hundred and twenty-seven acres of lush English countryside.

Dare made a derogatory sound in the back of his throat. 'Surely you're not considering it,' he dismissed. Because he couldn't think why she would. After the way the old man had hurt her, it was the last thing he deserved. And the last thing his mother should risk.

Unfortunately he could already tell that she was

not only considering the invitation, but that she wanted to go.

'The man's done nothing for you,' he reminded her, 'and now he wants to see you?' Dare knew he sounded contemptuous on her behalf and he was. 'He has an ulterior motive. You know that, right? He either needs money or he's dying.'

'Dare!' his mother exclaimed. 'I didn't realise I'd raised such a cynic.'

'Not a cynic, Ma, a realist.' He softened his voice. 'And I don't want you getting your hopes up that he's suddenly regretting his decision to cut you off all those years ago. Because if he's not dying it will be some kind of power play, mark my words.'

Dare knew he sounded harsh but someone had to look out for his mother, and he'd been doing it for so long now it had become second nature.

'He's my father, Dare,' she said softly. 'And he's reached out.' Her hands lifted and then fell back into her lap. 'I can't explain it really but it just feels like something I should do.'

Dare was a man who dealt in facts, not feelings, and as far as he was concerned his grandfather, Benson Granger, Baron Rothmeyer, was offering far too little far too late.

His mother could have used his help years ago. She didn't need him now.

'He mentioned that he's tried to find me before,' she said.

'He couldn't have tried very hard. You didn't exactly hide out.'

'No, but I have a feeling your father might have had something to do with that.'

Dare's eyes narrowed. He hated thinking about his father, let alone talking about him. 'Why do you say that?'

'Once when you were young and I still believed in him he said he'd made sure my father would always understand what he'd lost. I didn't think much of it at the time but now I wonder what prompted him to say that. And you know my father had no idea that you even existed until I mentioned it.'

'Well, he'll know I exist if you decide to take up his invitation because you won't be going alone.'

'So you think I *should* go?'

'Hell no. I think you should delete the email and pretend you never received it.'

His mother sighed. 'You're one of his heirs, Dare.'

Dare scowled. 'I don't care about that. I have no

interest in inheriting some old pile of rubble that probably costs more money to run than it's worth.'

'Rothmeyer House is very beautiful but…I can't help but think I made a mistake keeping you away from him after your father died. He is your only remaining relative on my side of the family besides your uncle, and your cousin, Beckett.'

Dare rounded the desk and took his mother's tightly clasped hands in his. 'Look at me, Ma.' He waited for her to raise her blue eyes to his. 'You did the right thing. I don't need him. I never did.'

'He changed after my mother died,' she said softly as if remembering something painful. 'He was never the most demonstrative man, but he became almost reclusive. Distant with everyone.'

Dare raised a brow. 'He sounds like a real gem.'

That brought a smile to his mother's lips, softening the deep lines on either side of her mouth and making her look more like her relaxed self. At fifty-four she was still a strikingly attractive woman, and finally seemed to have embraced life again and shaken off the many tough years she'd had to endure.

Which was one of the reasons Dare resented this communication from her estranged father now. His mother was happy and didn't need any reminders of the past; which was called the past for a reason.

'And our estrangement wasn't all his fault,' she continued softly. 'I was impetuous back then and…in the end he was right about your father and I was too proud to admit it.'

'You can't possibly blame yourself.' Dare frowned.

'No, I don't, but…' She looked up at him. 'You know, it's the strangest thing but right before he emailed me I started having dreams that I was back in the house. It's almost like a premonition, don't you think?'

Dare believed in premonitions about as much as he believed in fairytales.

'What I think is that you probably need closure. And I'll support you any way I can. Even going with you if that's what you want.'

She beamed him a smile. 'I was hoping you'd say that because after I mentioned you, he said he'd like to meet you.'

Great, Dare thought, just what he needed: a family reunion. 'When is this lunch?' he asked.

'Tomorrow.'

'Tomorrow!'

'Sorry, darling, I should have given you more

warning, but I wasn't sure I was even going to accept until today.'

Dare still wished she hadn't, but his mind was already turning to the logistics. 'Who else will be there?'

'I don't know.'

'Has he remarried? Do you have a stepmother, by chance?' His lips twisted cynically.

'No, but he did say he had a guest staying with him.'

'A woman?'

His mother shrugged. 'He didn't say. Our communication has been a little formal up to this point.'

'It doesn't matter,' Dare dismissed. 'I'll have Nina rearrange my diary.' He frowned. 'We'll leave at—'

His mother shook her head. 'I promised Tammy I'd see her in Southampton later today and I can't cancel on her. Why don't I meet you at Rothmeyer House tomorrow just before twelve?'

'If that's what you want.' He sat down at his desk. 'I've organised Mark to drive you today. I'll ask him to stay overnight to make things easier.'

'Thank you, Dare. You know I couldn't have asked for a better son, don't you?'

He stood up as she approached his desk and he enfolded her in his arms. 'And you know I'd do anything for you.'

'Yes, I know. And I appreciate it.'

Sensing a lingering sadness in her voice, Dare wondered if she was thinking about his father. Thinking about what a roller-coaster ride it had been with him right up until his death when Dare had just turned fifteen.

At best his father could be called a drifter chasing one dream after another in search of the big time, at worst he had been a conman with feet of clay. The only valuable lesson Dare had ever learnt from him was how to spot a con at fifty paces.

But it had been a good lesson that had helped Dare make more money than he could ever have imagined. And he had imagined a lot growing up in the poorest suburb in a small American town.

It had also stood him well when it came to relationships. For a while Dare had run with a rough crowd, but he'd soon learned that brothers were only brothers as long as you toed the line.

Since Dare didn't like toeing anyone else's line but his own, he kept to himself and trusted very few people.

Finding out when he was eighteen that his mother had an aristocratic lineage had only been interesting in that it had made Dare even more resentful of the family who had turned her away, thus forcing her to take three jobs just to make do. He'd never wanted to meet any of them and he still didn't.

But meet them he would and it wouldn't be tomorrow when his mother turned up for lunch. It would be today. This afternoon.

If Benson Granger thought he could insinuate himself into Dare's mother's life for any reason other than an altruistic one, he had another think coming.

And while it wasn't at all convenient to take a trip to Cornwall that afternoon, it would give him a chance to take his new toy out on the open roads.

Dare smiled, but it wasn't the charming, devil-may-care smile that made women swoon and men envious. It was a hunter-with-his-prey-in-his-sights smile, and for the first time since his mother had given him the disturbing news Dare thought he might actually enjoy setting his grandfather straight on a few things.

* * *

The locals at Rothmeyer village said that the summer they were having was the best in the last thirty years. Warm, balmy days, and light, breezy nights straight out of a Beatrix Potter fable.

Up at Rothmeyer House, the grand estate that bordered one side of the village, Carly Evans braced her spent arms on the edge of the deep blue swimming pool and hauled her tired body out of the water.

'Whoever said they got an endorphin rush out of exercise was either lying or dead,' she muttered to no one but the Baron's Pekinese, who snapped at passing insects as he lay like an untidy mop in the shade of the terrace.

Carly had been doing laps of the pool and jogging during her free time at Rothmeyer House since she'd arrived three weeks ago and she'd yet to feel anything other than exhausted and sore.

Not that she should be complaining on a day like today. Or any day. Working as the elderly Baron Rothmeyer's temporary doctor had been a real coup. Not only was the location spectacular, but, due to the Baron having to undergo a life-threatening operation in two weeks, it was also live-in. As in, living in the main house, live-in.

But the job would be over soon and she'd have to move on. Which was fine with Carly who, much to her parents' distress, had become something of a wandering gypsy this past year.

She pulled a face at the thought and squeezed water out of her long red hair, flicking it back over her shoulder. She was about as much like a gypsy as a nun was a circus performer, and up until a year ago she had led a very conventional life as a hard-working doctor in one of Liverpool's best hospitals.

That was until the bottom had fallen out of her world and ruined everything.

Grabbing a towel, Carly briskly swiped at her face and body. She grabbed her phone and settled onto a lounger, determined that with the Baron gone for another few hours she was not going to waste her free time thinking about the past.

'If you don't face things,' her father had said, 'they become mountains instead of molehills.'

As far as Carly was concerned hers had started out as a mountain and when it became a molehill she might consider returning home. Which was just as hard for her as it was her loving family because at heart Carly was a homebody who loved her parents. And her sister.

A familiar lump formed in her throat as the past lurched into her consciousness.

To distract herself she grabbed her cell phone. She had one new email from her parents, who would no doubt be subtly trying to find out if she really was okay, one from her old alma mater, and another from her temp agency, Travelling Angels.

Clicking to open her work email, she read that they had another job lined up for her as soon as this one was finished and did she want it. Being one of only three fully qualified doctors on their roster, she had so far not been without work. Which was fine with Carly. Busy meant less time for contemplating past mistakes.

But she wasn't ready to think about her next move yet so she closed that email and tapped on the one from her parents. Yes, there it was, the question of when they would see her next, and whether she'd made any decisions about her future.

Carly sighed and closed that email as well.

A year ago her beautiful, kind and gregarious sister had died of a rare and aggressive form of leukaemia. To add insult to injury, Carly's über-successful boyfriend had been cheating on her instead of being by her side to support her.

Not that she'd really turned to Daniel for support during those months. Being an important cardiologist, he was generally busy and, if she was being honest with herself, their relationship had never been like that.

He had pursued her because he respected her and she had accepted his invitation to go out because she'd been flattered by his attention. Then Liv had become sick and everything had fallen apart. Daniel had become resentful of the time she spent with her sister, questioning her about her movements at every turn and accusing her of cheating on him and using her sister as a ruse.

No matter what she had said, he hadn't believed her and then she'd discovered that in fact he had been the one cheating on her. On top of all that, everyone at her hospital had known about it and no one had said a word to her. The whole experience had been mortifying.

Feeling the sun burning into her skin, Carly yanked on a pair of cut-off denim shorts, dislodging the slender black velvet jeweller's box that had arrived for her earlier that day.

Still not quite believing what was inside, she opened it and once more marvelled at the divinely expensive ruby necklace nestled against the royal blue silk lining.

'*To match your hair,*' the card had read, followed by a swirling signature that denoted the sense of importance Benson's grandson, Beckett Granger, cloaked himself in.

Carly shook her head as she took out the necklace. For a start her hair was more orange than ruby red so if Beckett had thought to impress her with his cleverness he'd be disappointed.

If he thought to impress her with the amount he must have spent on it he'd be disappointed as well. Carly was too practically minded for lavish jewellery and still wore the diamond stud earrings her parents had bought her ten years ago, much to Liv's disgust.

But she did have to give him points for his approach. The necklace was undoubtedly the most expensive attempt a man had ever made to get her attention and she'd had a few offers over the years. Some had been patients, or relatives of patients, others had been doctors—but Benson's pompous grandson had taken the cake.

Even if she weren't still getting over a bad relationship with a doctor with a God complex she would never have gone for Beckett. There was something a little bit slimy about the man. He also had a sense of entitlement a mile wide and at one point, when she'd declined yet another invitation to dinner, she'd been sure he'd been about to stamp his foot.

Since Benson didn't want anyone to know about his illness, Beckett believed her to be the daughter of an important friend of his grandfather's but that hadn't stopped him from cornering her one night when he'd been two drinks past his limit. His attempt at seducing her had been more a nuisance than anything else, and Carly felt sure he would have been embarrassed about it the following morning.

It also spoke volumes that Benson trusted his staff with the information about his illness, but not his own grandson.

Still, the man could have been a god amongst men and she wouldn't have accepted his attention. She hadn't exactly sworn off men for ever, but she couldn't think of anything worse than adding a man into her complicated life right now. Not with the poor judgment she'd shown in the past.

Her father assured her that all she needed was a plan to get her back on track, maybe finish her surgical studies, but Carly wasn't even sure she wanted to remain in the medical profession, let alone become a surgeon.

The ruby necklace lay heavy in her palm, the sun hot on her shoulders. She'd have to get it back to him as soon as possible, but, while Beckett had entrusted it to the postal service, Carly wasn't so trusting. She'd much rather hand it back in person.

Spying her cotton shirt under a nearby lounge chair, Carly was about to fetch it when Gregory started yapping as if the grim reaper were bearing down on him.

Carly frowned at the pretentious little dog. All her life she'd brought home orphaned children and injured animals to take care of, her mother even complaining that she would save a caterpillar from a broccoli stalk if she'd let her, but when it came to Benson's prized Pekinese she had to admit she struggled. The pampered pooch had more of a sense of entitlement than Beckett, but she supposed it wasn't entirely his fault. Not with the way Benson doted on him.

'Okay, Gregory,' she said to him, 'you're going to bring the fire brigade if you keep making that racket.' She frowned as he pulled against his leash. 'What's got you so riled up anyway, boy?'

He was looking off towards the forest and Carly

made the mistake of following his gaze because while her gaze was averted he did his funny little twist manoeuvre she'd been warned about and slipped his collar.

'Gregory. No,' Carly called in frustration. 'I mean heel. Dammit,' she muttered as the dog tore off across the lime-green lawn, his caramel and black coat flying back in the breeze. 'Come back here!'

The last thing she needed was the Baron's beloved pet getting lost right before his operation. She'd never forgive herself.

Muttering a string of curse words, she shoved her feet into her flip-flops and took off after the cantankerous animal.

Halfway across the lawn she was glad she'd been exercising because she was gaining on him when he ducked through a border of shrubs and into the forested area. Cursing her bad luck, she vowed she'd give him to Mrs Carlisle to make potluck soup with when she got him.

The Baron would never complain about tofu again!

The thought made her smile. He'd been complaining about her menu plan ever since she'd arrived, trying to convince her that French fries and battered fish were fine in moderation for a man in his condition.

'Gregory, you little pain in the backside.' Carly shoved low-hanging branches aside and tried not to scratch her bare arms and legs any more than she had. 'If you get prickles in your coat I'll send you to that nasty dog groomer again! Gregory, dammit, come on, there's a good boy.' She tried to inject warmth into that last command but she wasn't sure he bought it.

A slight movement had her turning left and she stopped at the edge of a clearing. A family of rabbits lay sunning themselves on a small patch of grass as if they didn't have a care in the world. It was so lovely she forgot about Gregory until he burst out from behind an old oak tree like a bullet from a gun, scaring the daylights out of her and the unsuspecting rabbits.

'Gregory, no,' Carly shouted, rushing after him. The rabbits scattered, the largest—most likely the mother—dashing through the brush. Cursing the cranky dog for real now, Carly tried to keep pace with them. No way was he going to kill the mother rabbit on her watch.

In no mood to chase the Baron's insubordinate dog, Carly didn't hear the gunmetal-grey motorcycle bearing down on her around the bend in the driveway until it was too late. In what seemed like slow motion she realised that she wasn't going to be able to stop her forward momentum in time and, irrelevantly, that she was going to die with Beckett's silly necklace still gripped in her hand.

Half waiting for the sleek machine to barrel into her, Carly skidded on the gravel and landed on her bottom, rolling down the grassy embankment that ran alongside the road.

Winded, she lay unmoving, blinking dazedly up at the china-blue sky above.

She heard a choice curse word before a male head abruptly blocked out the light. The man was little more than a huge outline against the bright sun and then he went down on bended knee, leaning over her.

If she'd thought she was breathless before it was nothing compared to how she felt staring up into eyes so strikingly blue she could still have been staring at the sky. Combine those with chestnut hair that curled forward over his forehead, a square jaw, and strong nose and he had the kind of face Carly bemusedly thought she could look at for ever.

'Don't move.' He had quite the voice too. Deep

and low with just the right amount of authority to it. Which surely explained why she did exactly as he bade.

It wasn't until his large hands ran down her arms and over her legs that she tore her eyes from the way his black leather jacket hugged his wide shoulders and impressive chest.

'What are you doing?' she asked.

'Checking if you've broken anything.' The cold censure in his voice immediately put her back up.

'Are you a doctor?'

'No.'

She hadn't really expected that he would be— she'd never met a doctor encased in black leather before. 'I'm fine,' she huffed, not really sure if she was but, heck, she *was* a doctor!

'Keep still,' he growled as she struggled up onto her elbows.

'I said I'm fine.' She pushed at his hand on her leg and he rocked back on his heels. Carly could feel her heart beating hard behind her chest as he silently surveyed her.

'Good,' he finally said, standing up so that he once again towered over her. 'Perhaps you can explain what the hell you were doing running across the road like that. You could have been killed.'

Carly glanced at the sleek motorcycle waiting in the middle of the road like something out of a Batman movie. A flash of the motorcycle skidding in a graceful arc right before hitting her made her stomach pitch. The man had been riding that thing as if he were in the Indie 1000—or whatever that silly race was called—and now he wanted to make it her fault?

'Really?' she murmured pleasantly. 'If *I* could have been killed it was only because *you* were driving like a maniac on a narrow, unpaved road.'

Dare gazed down at the redheaded goddess spitting fire at him from eyes that were too grey to be green and too green to be grey. Olive perhaps.

'I was hardly driving like a maniac.' He'd barely been pushing fifty.

'Yes, you were *and* you were also on your phone!'

She said the last with wide eyes as if he'd been traversing a high wire at the same time.

'Don't get hysterical,' he told her. 'I wasn't on the phone. I was checking my GPS.' And in complete control the whole time.

'You had a phone in your hand while you were on a motorcycle! That's illegal!'

'Calm down, would you? I handled it.'

'Only just. And it's still illegal!'

Dare glanced down at her skimpy attire, a smile entering his voice. 'So what are you going to do? Arrest me?'

She glared up at him as if she'd like to do exactly that but not in the way he'd just been imagining. 'Who are you anyway?' she said haughtily.

He felt like saying the big bad wolf, given her snooty tone, but a better question was who was she? He glanced again at her cut-off denims and bright pink swimsuit that should have clashed with her bright hair but somehow didn't, immediately dismissing the notion that she was his elderly grandfather's guest. She looked more like the pool girl. The very *hot* pool girl. 'Who's asking?'

Her lips pursed into a flat line. 'I am.' She went to push up to her feet and paused when Dare automatically stuck his hand out to assist her. It didn't surprise him when she tried to ignore his offer of help but Dare was in no mood to put up with some holier-than-thou woman who had just taken a few years off his life when she'd come flying out of the trees and into his path.

'Take it,' he growled, grabbing onto her elbow as she tried to avoid him.

The way she wrenched her arm out of his grip as soon as she was vertical made his teeth gnash together.

'I don't need your help.'

'Listen, lady, it's only thanks to my quick reflexes that you're still here at all. You could show a little gratitude.'

'Don't you "lady" me. It's thanks to your crappy driving that I now have a sore—' She stopped as his eyes followed her hands to her bottom as she brushed it off.

He arched a brow. 'Behind?'

'Never mind,' she said primly.

'How did you not hear the bike anyway?'

'This is a private lane and I was chasing after a dog.' She gave his bike a contemptible glance. 'I was hardly expecting Evel Knievel to come barrelling down the road.'

'A dog, huh?' Dare unzipped his jacket and planted his hands on his hips. 'What kind of dog?'

He noticed she was staring at his chest, then his flat abdomen, and finally his zipper and heat poured through him as if she'd actually touched him.

As if sensing his visceral reaction to her she

started inching away from him as if he were some would-be rapist and he scowled.

'Yes.' Her voice had grown husky and she cleared it. 'A very big dog, if you must know.'

If she used her brain, Dare thought with rising annoyance, she'd realise that if he was going to grab her he wouldn't be standing around arguing with her.

But even as he thought it his eyes dropped to her high breasts pushing up against the straps of her one-piece suit and those long, lightly tanned legs shown to glorious perfection in cut-off denims. He'd seen many girls dressed similarly on a hot summer's day in his youth but he was quite sure he'd never seen legs as good as hers.

'What are you looking at?'

His eyes lifted to hers. Moss green, he decided, and full of awareness of how appreciative he had been of her figure.

'Your legs.' He smiled. 'You have them on display. You can hardly blame a man for looking.'

'Excuse me?' Her eyes shot daggers at him and he supposed he deserved it. He wasn't here to come on to the pool girl and he was hardly desperate for female company.

'Listen—'

'How dare you?' She stabbed a slender finger at his chest. 'I'm wearing a bathing suit because it's hot and I've just been for a swim.'

'And you were looking for a dog. I get it. But—'

'Not that I need to explain myself to the likes of you,' she vented.

Dare's eyes narrowed dangerously. 'The likes of me?'

'That's what I said. Are you hard of hearing? Oh, no!' She gave a cry of dismay. 'My necklace!' She turned quickly, her russet cloud of hair swinging around her shoulders. 'I can't have lost it.'

Dare sighed. He was tired after driving hours to get here on top of already putting in what felt like a full day at the office, and in no mood to be insulted by some sexy little shrew. 'What does it look like?'

'It's a ruby pendant, on a gold—'

'This it?'

He reached into the longer grass where it circled a bush. He'd noticed a glint of something before when he'd first rushed over to her and now held a very expensive little trinket in the palm of his hand. He let out a low whistle of appreciation. She definitely wasn't just the pool girl if this was hers.

Dare flashed a smile. 'A pretty piece. I'm not

sure it goes with the outfit though.' She stiffened as he looked her over. 'Might I suggest a string bikini next time?'

'I wasn't wearing it,' she said hotly. 'It was a gift.'

Dare laughed. 'I hardly thought you paid for it yourself, baby.' In his experience no woman would.

She stared at him mouth agape and he supposed he had sounded a touch derogatory but...

'Did you really just call me *baby*?'

Yeah, he had. For some reason discovering the necklace had made his mood take another dive. 'Look—'

'Listen? Look?' Her finger stabbed in his direction again. 'You are one condescending piece of work, *darling*.' She stepped forward, her cheeks pink with annoyance. 'Give me that.' She reached for the necklace in his hand but Dare reacted instinctively and raised it above his head. She was medium to tall in height but there was no way she was close to his six feet four.

Realising it, she pulled up short, her hands flattening against his white T-shirt to stop herself from falling against him. Her eyes grew wide, her soft mouth forming a perfect 'O', and his eyes lingered before returning to hers.

Dare would have said the whole 'time standing still' thing was just hogwash, but right then he couldn't hear a leaf rustling, or a bird calling, his mind empty of everything that didn't include getting her naked and horizontal as soon as possible.

Instinctively his free hand came around to draw her closer when the sound of yapping at his feet broke the spell. Disconcerted, Dare looked down into the upturned face of an ugly little mutt the size of a cat with its tongue hanging out. He grinned. 'This the big dog you were chasing?'

The redhead stepped back and threw him a filthy look as she reached for the small dog that danced just out of her reach.

'Gregory,' she growled in a warning voice. 'Heel.'

Dare would have laughed at her futile attempts to stay the dog if he hadn't been feeling so out of sorts.

'Here.' He held the necklace out impatiently as she made to run after the dog. 'Don't forget your gift.'

Turning on him with a malevolent look, she snatched the necklace from his hand and took off after the mutt. He doubted he'd have cause to see her again but strangely he found he wanted to.

Shaking his head, he walked back to his bike and shoved his helmet on, dismissing the pool girl from his mind as he gunned the engine and headed to the main house.

CHAPTER TWO

DARE PACED BACK and forth in what he surmised was a parlour room inside the grand house. He'd never been particularly good at cooling his heels and finding his grandfather out when he'd first arrived had turned an already grim mood further south. Two hours later it was fair to say it had hit rock bottom. He wondered if it was a tactical move on his grandfather's behalf because Dare had presumed to turn up unannounced a day earlier than he was expected.

Glancing around the elegant room, he took in the heavily oak-panelled walls dating back to the sixteenth century. Like the bedroom he'd been shown to earlier to 'freshen up'—which had most likely been code for ditching his leathers—the antique furniture was graceful and well-appointed. Given the state of the rest of the house and grounds that Dare had seen, he surmised that money wasn't behind the old man's invitation to his mother. Which left the possibility that he was ill and/or dying.

The thought didn't stir an ounce of emotion in Dare at all. But the line of oil paintings mounted high on the walls? They were most likely his ancestors, he thought with distaste, and they gave him the creeps. He steeled himself against the unexpected need to search out a likeness. He was nothing like these people and never would be.

It was hard to imagine his mother running around here as a child. The place might be majestic and steeped in history, but it was completely devoid of laughter and lightness. And so alien to his own impoverished upbringing. Not that the wealth of the place bothered him. He could buy it a thousand times over if he wanted to.

He checked his watch, impatient to meet the old man who had unsettled his mother's world once more. And his own, if the truth be told.

'I apologise for keeping you waiting, sir.' The butler who had shown him to his room earlier tipped his head as he stepped into the parlour.

Dare smiled at the man's cordiality, but it didn't reach his eyes. Fed up with waiting in his room like a good little schoolboy, Dare had prowled around the house on his own, finally being shown into this room by one of the servants.

'Forget it,' Dare said. His quarrel wasn't with the butler so why make his life harder by being a jerk?

'May I fix you a pre-dinner drink, sir?'

Dare turned away from a life-sized oil painting of a man in a bad wig. 'Scotch. Thank you.'

He had no intention of staying for dinner but the butler didn't need to know that either.

Dare gazed around at the book-lined walls, softly lit lamps, and matching damask sofas. A tartan throw rug caught his eye, the mix of autumn colours reminding him of the pool girl's glorious mane of hair. She'd been absolutely beautiful, wild and pagan with that long, unbound mane splayed out against the bright green grass, and then she'd opened her eyes and he'd been jolted by the greyish-green hue that reminded him of the Spanish moss that grew on many of the trees back home. The combination was startling. Then there was her skin that had been creamy and, oh, so inviting to touch.

She had reminded him of the angel he and his mother used to place on top of their Christmas tree when he was a child. Her temper, though, had definitely not been angelic and his lips quirked as he recalled how her eyes had shot sparks at him whenever he'd riled her.

Something about her had made him want to get her all hot and bothered, even when she'd insulted him. Not that he had any time for the pool girl, he reminded himself. But still…he had no doubt as to how good those sweet curves of hers would have felt in his arms.

Catching the ludicrousness of his thoughts, Dare gave himself a mental slap-down. He was thirty-two years old, long past the age of mentally drooling about how a woman would feel in his arms. How she would taste on his lips. How he might find her once this business with his grandfather was done.

He took a swig of his drink. He was long past the age of chasing after women as well. Not that he'd ever had to do much of that. He'd always been good with his hands and had a strong attention to detail and the women had loved him for it. True, they often complained that he put work ahead of them, but he'd never claimed to be perfect.

He wondered yet again who had given the pool girl the expensive bauble she'd been so afraid she'd lost. No doubt a lover, but who? His grandfather?

He nearly sprayed his Scotch at the thought. As if a gorgeous woman like that would have anything to do with a decrepit, old man.

A light sound outside the door caught his attention and he looked up as a white-haired, elegantly dressed gentleman entered the room.

Finally...

Dare took his grandfather all in at once. The tall build and broad shoulders, the lined face that was both proud and strong. He'd somehow expected his grandfather to look frail and sick and the fact that he didn't was as irritating to him as his thoughts about the redhead.

Both men took a moment to appraise the other, Dare giving nothing away beneath the old man's regard.

Let him look, he thought, *and let him understand that I am not the weak man my father was. I don't run from my responsibilities.*

'Dare.' His grandfather said his name with an air of familiarity that rankled. 'I'm so very pleased to meet you at last. Please forgive my absence when you first arrived. I would have rearranged my afternoon plans had I known you were arriving earlier.'

Dare didn't respond. He had no intention of pretending any form of civility with this man who had thrown his mother out all those years ago.

His mouth tightened, his attention drawn to a subtle movement behind the old man. When he saw it was the pool girl it took all his effort to keep his expression implacable.

His eyes moved down the length of her. The wild, pagan angel was nowhere in sight. In her place stood a very regal, very sophisticated young woman in a simple knee-length black dress and high heels, her rich red hair swept back into a tight knot at the base of her skull. Not many women could wear a hairdo that severe. She could.

Her moss-green eyes returned his regard coolly and a muscle jumped in his jaw. She wasn't the pool girl, that was for sure, which left the only other conclusion he had arrived at front and centre in his mind.

But surely not…

His grandfather turned to acknowledge her presence, his hand hovering at the small of her back as he guided her forward. 'Please allow me to introduce you to Carly Evans. Carly, this is my grandson, Dare James.'

She gave his grandfather a quizzical glance and

Dare's jaw clenched at the unspoken communication between the two.

But surely yes…

This was definitely his grandfather's mystery guest.

He could barely believe it was true. He was so caught off guard he nearly missed the way her eyes dropped nervously from his as she stepped forward to greet him. 'Mr James.' Her smile was a little tremulous and he was somehow gratified by her nervousness. He bet she wouldn't insult him now. 'I'm pleased to meet you.'

God, she really was stunning and he didn't like the jolt of adrenaline that coursed through his blood at the sight of her. 'Ms Evans, it's a delight to see you again.'

Her eyes cut back to his with surprise. So she hadn't told his grandfather about their meeting. How very interesting.

'You've already met?' Surprise crossed his grandfather's craggy features as well and Dare was glad he wasn't the only one in the room who was thrown off course here.

'We ah…met earlier,' the goddess hedged, her face blushing prettily. 'I didn't realise he was your grandson at the time. For some reason I thought he'd be younger. And English instead of American.'

There was only one reason a beautiful young woman would be sleeping with an old man like his grandfather and it left a sour taste in Dare's mouth.

He remembered one time at Harvard when a woman had been playing both he and his room-mate at the same time. They'd both ditched her as soon as they found out. Dare had laughed that she'd wanted Liam for his money and Dare for his sexual prowess. Then they'd spent hours over beers arguing the point and debating the moral-ity of women on the make.

No need to debate this woman's morality. It was staring him in the face. Or rather gazing adoringly at his grandfather.

'Perhaps you would have been a little nicer if you had known who I was,' he suggested, want-ing to ruffle her smooth feathers as she had ruf-fled his.

Her eyes narrowed. 'I wasn't rude.'

Dare's brow rose. 'You were hardly welcom-ing, if I recall.'

'You nearly ran me down.'

'Ran you down?' His grandfather's brow furrowed with concern.

'I got a fright when I didn't hear the motorcycle...it was nothing,' she assured him gently.

'Then why bring it up?' Dare asked pleasantly.

She frowned at him. 'I didn't. You did.'

'Carly, are you sure you're okay?' His grandfather's concern was like an annoying splinter under the skin.

'Absolutely. Gregory broke his leash again and when I went to get him I wasn't concentrating well enough.'

'A woman who admits fault; be still my beating heart,' Dare mocked softly.

She shot him a fiery look that left scorch marks across the silk rug between them. Dare smiled and watched, transfixed as she collected herself and reinstated her sophisticated façade. The transformation was quite something to behold.

'I apologise if you thought I was in any way rude, Mr James,' she said, as if a poker were rammed up her delectable backside. 'It was not my intention.'

Not now that she knew who he was, anyway. She wouldn't want to do anything to unsettle her gravy train.

'Is that right?' he said smoothly.

Her face coloured again and her little chin went up at the challenging note in his voice.

He trapped her gaze with his. *Don't mess with me, my little beauty*, he silently warned. *You'll lose.*

She blinked as if to say she had no idea what he was on about and he nearly applauded her for her acting skills.

Instead he dismissed her and set his chilly gaze on his grandfather. 'Why is she here?'

His grandfather shifted uncomfortably. 'Carly and I have taken to having a drink before dinner and as I wasn't expecting you until tomorrow I invited her to join us. I hope you don't mind.'

For reasons he didn't want to examine, Dare did. Very much. 'And if I do?' He asked, sipping his Scotch.

His deceptively amiable question froze the cool smile on Carly's face.

His grandfather frowned. 'Carly is…well, she's a guest of mine,' he finished lamely.

'How nice for you.' Dare ran his hand over the length of the tartan rug, noting the frown on Carly Evans's face as he did so.

'I can go.' She moistened her lips with a nervous flicker of her pink tongue. 'I don't mind, really—'

'Stay,' Dare said, rethinking his position. It might actually be better to have her around to get a full picture of what was going on.

Her eyes darkened infinitesimally at the command. She obviously liked to be the one in charge.

So did he.

His grandfather cleared his throat to cut through the awkward silence and Dare watched him move to the drinks trolley. 'Cointreau on ice, Carly?'

'No, thank you,' she husked, moving forward. 'I'll just have water but, here, let me get it. You sit down.'

The lady had expensive taste, Dare thought, but then he knew that from the ruby necklace, which was markedly absent. In fact she wasn't wearing any jewellery to speak of. Had she not had time to put it on?

He watched as she fixed her own drink and poured tonic water for Benson without having to ask what he would like. How very *comfortable* it all was. The nubile, young woman playing up to the doddery old rich fool no doubt hoping he'd kick the bucket soon. Dare couldn't help but acknowledge that he was disappointed. He'd somehow felt she had more substance to her.

Yeah, right. Substance. Was that what he was calling lust these days?

Nothing like a cold shot of reality to kill that bird dead.

He glanced at her ring finger. No diamond rock there. Obviously she still had some work to do yet.

He felt something primitive unfurl inside him. Something dark and dangerous. Disgust, he told himself. Every one of his senses had gone on high alert as soon as she had entered the room and he didn't like it that he was so aware of her as a woman. Not when she was screwing his grandfather.

Just the thought of the two of them intimate made his stomach turn. Could a man even get it up at that age? A cynical smile touched the corner of Dare's mouth. He certainly hoped so.

But he wasn't here to think about his grandfather's sordid sex life, he reminded himself. He was here to find out why Benson had contacted his mother, and he wouldn't let himself get sidetracked by this wide-eyed mistress again.

'As pleasant as this is,' Dare mocked, facing off

against his grandfather, 'what I want to know is why you contacted my mother.'

A heavy silence followed his lethally soft words and it sent a chill down Carly's spine.

When Benson had informed her that his grandson would be joining them for drinks Carly had thought he had meant Beckett, and she'd been pleased that she would be able to return his necklace to him and not have to worry about losing it.

Now she wished that it *had* been Beckett, because she had no idea how to deal with this arrogant American's barely veiled hostility. She especially had no idea how to deal with the way her insides jolted with nervous heat every time he trained his piercing blue eyes on her.

The Baron inclined his head towards his grandson, a small sigh escaping past his lips. 'I didn't imagine this would be easy.'

Carly noted the aggressive stance in the younger man. He might now only be wearing faded denim jeans and a white T-shirt but he looked no less intimidating for it. In fact he looked even more so because now she could see that he was as leanly muscled as she had first imagined. And with black biker boots on his feet...

'What did you imagine it would be?' Dare asked the Baron with cold disdain.

'Difficult,' he acknowledged wryly.

'Glad to see you're a realist.' His gaze homed in on the Baron like a shooter lining up a clay pigeon. 'At first I thought you needed money but given the appearance of the place I've discounted that. Which leaves the possibility that you're sick or dying. Not that you look it.'

A gasp escaped Carly before she could contain it. 'That is so rude,' she admonished, welcoming the bite of her temper in replace of her previous uncertainty.

Dare's lethal gaze swung to hers, pinning her to the spot. 'I'm sorry,' he said softly, 'what made you think I was talking to you?'

Oh! Carly refused to let him intimidate her. The Baron was her patient and it was her job to make sure he was well enough to undergo surgery to remove a brain tumour the size of a golf ball in two weeks' time. He needed rest and relaxation, not animosity and outright aggression.

She would probably be able to add heart attack to his list of ailments if his grandson continued on in this vein.

'You shouldn't speak to anyone like that!' she reproved.

'It's all right, Carly.' The Baron patted her hand. 'Dare has a right to feel angry. And from what I understand my grandson has a reputation for being ruthless, powerful, and relentless when he wants something.' He listed the traits as if they were trophies to be shown off on a mantel, Carly thought with disgust. 'It actually pleases me that he feels the need to defend Rachel.'

Carly tried to accept the Baron's version of things. Rachel, she knew, was Dare's mother, but other than that she didn't know anything about their history.

Fortunately the butler chose that moment to enter quietly and announce that dinner was ready to be served.

'Very good, Roberts.' The Baron smiled, but Carly could see it was strained. 'Dare, I was hoping that you might join us for the evening meal.'

Carly couldn't believe he was extending an invitation, given the level of disrespect he had been shown.

'I hadn't intended to,' Dare said coldly, and Carly felt her shoulders relax slightly as he declined. 'But if it's okay with Miss Evans perhaps I will.'

If it was okay with her? Carly's spine snapped straight. *Why would he put this on her?*

'Of course it's all right with me,' she said, too brightly.

'Very good.' She felt the Baron's relief as he exhaled. 'Shall we adjourn to the dining room? I, for one, am very eager to find out what Mrs Carlisle has prepared in your honour, Dare, and I do so enjoy eating my food without indigestion. Roberts, if you would be so kind as to set another place at the table?'

'Very good, sir.'

For a moment Carly thought—*hoped*—that Dare was going to change his mind, but then he shrugged.

'I haven't eaten anything decent since breakfast. Lead the way, old man.'

She felt the Baron tense as he cupped her elbow and she wanted to strangle Dare James with her bare hands. She was quite sure that whatever bad blood was between these men it didn't warrant this level of disrespect.

Reminding herself that it really wasn't any of her business, and that she was here for the Baron and the Baron alone, Carly let him lead her out of the room, acutely aware of Dare's cold eyes on her as she moved past.

She was infinitely glad that she'd taken the time with her appearance before dinner. And she told herself that she hadn't done so on the off chance that she'd run into this horrible stranger again… she'd done it because…yes, okay, she had wondered if she'd run into him in passing and she'd somehow felt that she'd need armour if she did. Well, she'd certainly got that right. And she had no idea how she was going to make it through a whole dinner if the Baron's grandson didn't start playing nice.

'You've done well for yourself, Dare,' the Baron said as they were all seated at the large dining table.

'Unlike my loser father, you mean?'

The Baron sighed. 'I didn't mean to sound as if I was passing judgment.' He moved aside as a plate was placed in front of him. 'Though you do seem to have inherited your father's acerbic wit.'

Score one for the older gentleman, Carly thought, completely disconcerted when she glanced across the table to find Dare staring at her.

'That's not all I inherited,' Dare bit out tautly.

'Duck *à l'orange*,' the Baron said, inhaling the fragrance as the servant stepped back. 'My favourite.'

Carly gave him a secret smile. 'I do relent sometimes,' she teased.

'This is all very nice,' Dare bit out, not hiding the fact that he didn't think it was nice at all. 'But I didn't come here to discuss food or to make small talk.'

Tension crossed the table like laser beams.

'I can see that,' the Baron said. He put down his fork. 'What did you come for, Dare? To put me in my place?'

'It's no less than you deserve.'

'I'm not going to argue with you about that,' Benson said quietly, 'but you have to understand I've only recently become abridged of your father's death. And of the fact that Rachel must have struggled for years afterwards. That she even had a child. You!'

'And you think that entitles you to contact her?' Dare said with barely leashed fury. 'You rejected her. You kicked her out when she chose my father over your archaic expectations. But she doesn't need you now. She's doing fine.'

'Thanks to you,' Benson acknowledged softly.

'My mother is a strong woman with high morals. She would have made it fine without me.'

Completely shocked by Dare's revelations, Carly felt like an interloper with no idea how to ease the tension between the two men.

'Perhaps we should save this conversation for when we're alone.' The Baron touched Carly's hand as he spoke and she realised she had a forkful of food held halfway to her mouth. 'There's no need to ruin Carly's appetite, hmm?'

'But it was okay to ruin my mother's life?' Dare's gaze was harsh when it landed on her again and her heart thumped behind her breastbone. 'By all means.' He stabbed a morsel of food on his plate. 'Let's not upset the lovely Carly. Tell me, Miss Evans, how long have you known my grandfather?'

Clearing her throat, and glad for the opportunity to turn the conversation away from the Baron in case it ratcheted up his blood pressure, Carly smiled politely. 'A few months now.' She had met Benson at a nearby clinic when he'd first presented with breathing problems and when he'd learned she was temping he'd requested her services.

'And when did you move in?'

Distracted by his mesmerising blue eyes, she took a sip of her sparkling wine. 'Three weeks ago. I...' She stopped, realising that she was about to reveal the reason for her stay. 'I—'

'I know of Carly's family,' Benson cut in to save her. 'A happy coincidence really. Our ancestors fought together against the Jacobite Rebellion in 1715. Carly is the relative of a famous viscount.'

Dare curled his lip as if he couldn't have cared if she were directly in line to the throne. And her heritage hardly counted when she was the distant cousin of a cousin, and her family had lived a very humble existence for well over a century now.

'Excuse me, sir,' Roberts said, approaching Benson. 'A phone call has come through. I think you'll want to take it.'

'Fine, Roberts. Thank you.'

Looking irritated at the interruption, Benson pushed to his feet and took the hands-free phone proffered by the butler. He frowned in Carly and Dare's direction. 'I apologise for this interruption.'

As soon as the door closed behind him Carly was acutely aware of the antique clock ticking away in the corner of the room and the lean, powerful male regarding her across the table.

Dare James was too big, too sure of himself,

and too arrogant for her liking. Oh, he didn't exactly have Daniel's air of cultured superiority over others—something she hadn't noticed until Daniel had well and truly humiliated her—no, Dare's was more a latent power that drew the eye and let everyone around him know that he was in charge. Which was just as bad.

The T-shirt he wore did little to contain the bulge in his biceps and he looked as if he had the strength to rip a giant oak out of the ground and snap it in half. Right now he looked as if he wanted to snap her in half.

A shiver raced down her spine at the memory of those large hands skimming over her, leaving her hot and bothered. She'd attributed her earlier physical response to the heat of the day and her worry over Gregory muddling her senses. Now she knew that it was her feminine instincts signalling danger with capital letters and she was listening. This time, she was definitely listening.

'More wine, Miss Evans?'

Carly regarded him warily as he picked up the wine bottle. As tempted as she was to settle her sudden nervousness with more alcohol, Carly knew drinking any more would put her at a disadvantage with this man. 'No, thank you.' She cleared her throat, searching around her frazzled mind for something to say. 'So, is this your first time at Rothmeyer House?' she asked.

'You mean you don't know?'

'No,' she said politely, her mind still absorbing what she had heard about his family history. 'Should I?'

Dare watched her nibble on the corner of her lower lip and he almost felt sorry for her. Then he remembered why she was even here and felt like snarling. 'I would have thought so.'

'I can't imagine why.'

'So sweet,' he murmured, wondering if her lips would feel as soft as they looked.

She frowned. 'I can see that you're very upset with your grandfather but do you really think that coming over all macho and being aggressive is going to help the situation?'

'Oh, good,' he said. 'We finally get to the part of the evening where we give up pretending we have to be polite to each other.'

Carly stared at him in shocked silence and Dare nearly laughed. What did she expect? That he would welcome his grandfather's innocent little mistress into his life with open arms? Not likely.

'I wasn't aware that you had been polite,' she

mocked. 'I must have missed that brief moment in time.'

Dare laughed. 'You've got guts, I'll give you that.'

She frowned at him. 'Is this because I ran out in front of you on the road?' she asked. Her expression so sweetly confused he found himself wanting to be taken in by her.

'Try again,' he said, calling himself a fool.

'Try again?' She shook her head. 'I don't know what to try again. I have no idea why you're being so hostile towards me.'

'You think I'm hostile?'

He knew damned well he was being hostile, Carly thought. She took a deep breath and reminded herself that she was usually the doctor others called on to deal with belligerent patients. 'Yes, you're being hostile,' she said calmly.

'On the contrary, I don't think I've been hostile at all. But if it makes you feel better, then I'll try to fix it.'

Carly let out a relieved breath. 'Thank you.' She gave him a shaky smile. 'It's just that your grandfather is very…tired at the moment.'

'Oh, now that's just showing off, Red.'

Showing off? Red? Carly's teeth ground together at his mocking tone. 'It's a basic human kindness to be civil,' she reminded him. 'If he were a stranger on the street I'm sure you wouldn't say the things you have.'

'But he's not a stranger on the street. He's a wealthy old fool.' He smiled but it didn't reach his eyes. 'And while we're on the subject, I have to commend you on your fast work. You must have some very special attributes to get in here in under a month.'

Carly frowned. If this was him trying to be less hostile he needed to go see someone about it. 'What do you mean by fast work?'

'The innocent confusion is good,' he murmured. 'It's a real turn-on. But I'm quite sure you know that. Tell me, Miss Evans, do you like books?'

Carly blinked. 'Books?'

'Those things people used to read in print form, but now mostly download online.'

'I believe they still print books, Mr James,' she said, a glimmer of anger burning low in her stomach. 'But, yes, I like to read.'

'I'm being facetious, Red.' He smiled easily. 'I prefer non-fiction to fiction. You?'

Carly would prefer to be anywhere but having to look into his handsome face. 'Both are good,' she said warily, wondering where he was going with this.

'Personally I'm too straightforward for fiction. I don't like things that are made-up.'

'Well, it depends on the author's imagination,' Carly said, pushing a strand of hair that had come loose from her bun back behind her ear.

'Do you have a good one?' He ran the tip of his index finger along the long stem of his wineglass.

'Miss Evans?'

Carly blinked. 'Book?'

'Imagination?'

'I…I like to think so, but I'm not an author. I couldn't wri—'

'Helen Garner is an author I admire.'

'Who?'

'I wouldn't expect you to know who she is. She's Australian. Very literary. I lived in Australia for a while when I was young. Did you know that?'

'No.' Carly glanced at the door wishing the Baron would hurry up and return. 'Look, Mr James—'

'Call me Dare.'

Carly let out a breath. 'This is all very fascinating but—'

'My mother discovered Ms Garner's work first, but then I happened to study her at university.'

'University?' Her voice sounded shaky and she cleared it.

'Keep up, Red.' His smile was so phony she wouldn't be surprised if he pulled out a deck of tarot cards and started reading her fortune. 'A university is an institution one attends when they're looking to better themselves.'

'I know what a university is, Mr James,' she said from between her teeth. 'I'm just struggling to follow the conversation.'

'Don't worry your pretty little head about it. You have other great *qualities* that are far more important, but you know that, don't you?' His eyes held hers. 'Are you sure you won't have another drink? Benson's pulled out all stops with the wine.'

As she realised that he had only been amusing himself at her expense Carly's slowly simmering anger just met its point of ignition. 'I'm trying to be pleasant here,' she bit out.

Dare rose from his seat, wine bottle in hand. 'Believe me, Red, so am I.'

Like hell. She glared at him. 'Call me that name again and you won't like the consequences.'

Many children had tried while she'd been growing up and they'd got the wrong end of her temper every time.

'Is that a threat?' he mocked.

Carly took a deep breath and told herself not to let him get to her. Then she didn't care. 'I don't like what you've been implying,' she said, facing him squarely. 'Why not come right to the point if you're so straightforward?'

He rounded the table and prowled towards her. Carly had to fight every bone in her body not to get up and run.

'You picked up on that, huh?'

'On your veiled animosity?' She gave him a superior smile of her own. 'Even a small child would have found it hard to miss.'

'But then children are so perceptive. Do you want children, Red?'

He reached out and brushed the loose strand of her hair back behind her ear. Carly gasped, twisting in her seat to look up at him. 'You don't care if I want children or not,' she said, distracted by the way her skin tingled where his fingers had grazed it.

'Not really,' he agreed affably, leaning on the back of her chair. 'But if they're on your agenda you might want to consider Benson's age. He won't exactly be pitching a football with the youngster in the backyard. Not that the backyard isn't big enough. You made sure of that first, didn't you?'

Carly would speak but she wasn't sure she could pry her teeth apart to get words out.

If she wasn't mistaken this Neolithic fool had just accused her of being his grandfather's mistress. She wasn't sure what she thought was worse. The fact that he believed her to have been intimate with a man nearly three times her age, or that he thought her a gold-digger.

Incensed beyond all reason, Carly tried to shove her chair back but found she couldn't because he had effectively caged her by bracing his arms on either side of her chair, his palms flat on the tabletop.

'Temper, temper, Red.' His warm breath feathered across her ear. 'What will Benson think if he comes back and finds you all riled up?'

'Hopefully he'll kick you out!' She knew she'd said the wrong thing by the way his muscles bunched in his arms. Her earlier analogy with that tree came to mind and she swallowed heavily. But instead of breaking her in half he leaned closer.

'I wanted to kiss you today, Red.' She jumped

as something gently brushed the side of her face. His nose? 'Out there on that hot, dusty road.'

Carly struggled to swallow. 'No,' she said automatically.

'Oh, yes.'

Carly jerked sideways as he inhaled her scent but that only pressed her up against the solid mass of his opposite shoulder, giving him access to the line of her neck. He was so close she felt enveloped by his heady, male warmth. 'And you wanted to kiss me too.'

'No!' she denied, pulling herself together. 'You're a bigger fool than I first thought if you believe that.' She gave a short, sharp laugh to reinforce her words.

He sniffed behind her ear. 'You smell sweet.'

Every part of Carly froze except her pulse, which was racing. Was he about to kiss her? If he was…if he was she would…stop breathing.

'I'm right is what I am,' he murmured. 'I think you'd like me to do it even now with the old man in the next room. Should we give him a show?'

Before she could pick up the water jug and dump its contents over his insolent head the door to the dining room swung open. Dare slowly straightened, picked up the wine bottle, and poured her wine as if that were all he'd been doing all along.

Hot colour swept over Carly's face and she forced a smile to her lips.

'So sorry for the interruption,' Benson said, resuming his seat. 'That was Beckett.'

'How is he?' Carly asked, her voice pitched just a little too high. Really she couldn't care less about Beckett, but he was a safer topic than the man slowly making his way back to his seat as if nothing had just happened between them.

And nothing had, she reminded herself. He was taunting her, that was all, because he was a rude, callous individual with no manners whatsoever. What she wouldn't give to wipe that superior smile off his face and tell him she'd rather kiss a snake. Only he was a snake, she thought venomously. It was unfair of him to include her in his bad feelings for his grandfather. Making assumptions about her out of hand.

If she had wanted to bring him down a peg or two earlier, she wanted to even more now. Especially as he sat slouched back in his chair, gazing at her as if he were the king of the world. Well, he wasn't king of her world, and, oh, how she'd like to wipe that crooked grin from his face. He was enjoying her discomfort, damn him.

But to correct his nefarious assumptions would be to disclose her real reason for being here and she'd assured the Baron that she'd keep his secret for as long as he wanted to. And although she felt sure that Benson would be horrified at the conclusions his grandson had drawn she wasn't going to bring them up now.

And perhaps it would be better to let the arrogant Dare James labour under his misapprehensions about her.

Let him hang himself with them. The embarrassment he would no doubt feel at being so wrong about her—and his grandfather—would keep a smile on her face for days.

Yes. She let out a slow breath. She was going to enjoy watching this arrogant stranger squirm when he found out that, not only was she not a greedy little gold-digger, but that she was probably more qualified than he was.

University... She raised her wineglass in the air and gave him a small toast. She knew all about university and before she was finished with him he would know that she was a woman to look out for. A woman who was not going to be cowed by a man like him ever again.

And as for wanting to kiss him? She couldn't think of anything more revolting than having his smug mouth on hers.

She brought her glass to her lips, pleased with how steady and cool she felt, how detached. But then his gaze dropped to her mouth and her equilibrium wavered, all but disintegrating when the tip of his tongue came out to touch his bottom lip as if he was thinking about how she would taste.

It was a brief, subtle move but it set every one of her nerves on edge.

She had to force the cool liquid down past the lump in her throat without choking but she did it, and was pleased with herself until she realised that he was deliberately trying to put her off stride again. And it had worked. She now felt as if she were burning up from the inside out.

Damn him.

The man was beyond evil. He was a demon. The devil himself.

Fortunately the Baron chose that moment to break into their silent stand-off with a comment about the meal, which Carly had completely forgotten about.

She pushed the last of it around her plate as if her appetite hadn't fled, but then she noticed how pale Benson looked and could have kicked herself.

Concerned, she forgot all about his obnoxious grandson and clasped Benson's wrist. He gave her a wan smile, knowing that she was surreptitiously taking his pulse. One forty over eighty, at a guess. Not critical, but definitely too high for a man in his condition.

She gave him a warning squeeze. 'I think you should call it a night,' she advised softly. And she definitely wanted to. Anything to get away from the pointed glare of the man opposite her.

Dare watched the intimate little tableau play out before his eyes. The woman had no shame. No shame whatsoever, and his increasingly bad mood had nothing to do with the fact that he would like those slender fingers wrapped around a certain part of his anatomy, and where he was imagining was a long way from his wrist.

He didn't know what had possessed him to taunt her the way that he had, but it had very nearly backfired when he'd got a whiff of her light scent.

He breathed in deeply. He was pretty sure it was only shampoo he had smelt, shampoo and woman, and his recall was so strong she might as well have been sitting right beside him. Or in his lap.

A muscle jumped in his jaw and he realised he was clenching his teeth hard enough to break them. It pained him greatly that his body hardened in anticipation every time he looked at her. And when she spoke; that lilting English accent…he'd lived on and off in the country for about a year and never noticed what a turn-on it was.

At times she sounded exactly like a reprimanding English schoolmarm and at others as if she'd just climbed out of bed after being satisfied over and over. Add in that firecracker temper and haughty attitude and it was all he could do not to haul her across the table and find out if all that fire and ice translated to passion between the sheets. Or, on the table, rather, given their location.

Dare wondered what his grandfather would think if he told him it would take little more than the crook of his finger to have his mistress in his own bed.

The thought made him sick. He wasn't here for that. And he certainly wasn't here to compete with the old man. Let him make a fool of himself over a woman if that was his wont. Dare never had before and he never would.

Especially not over a woman like this. One with such a low moral compass. Which was probably why it bothered him so much that he found her so attractive. He just didn't understand it. He'd been exposed to a limitless amount of beautiful women since he'd reached puberty and even more since he'd made it rich. Women more beautiful than Carly Evans, and yet all evening he'd struggled to take his eyes off her.

Bottom line, he despised her for what she was and he despised himself for wanting her regardless.

'Goodnight, Mr James.'

'It's Dare,' he reminded her, holding out his hand even though he knew it would be a mistake to touch her again. He couldn't help himself it seemed, his legendary self-control a distant memory in her presence.

She hesitated, glancing at his hand, and he nearly smiled for real when good manners—of which, yes, his had been in short supply that evening—determined that she must.

Immediately he raised it to his lips. 'Sleep well.' *Or not*, his eyes said.

Hers widened as if she read him loud and clear before giving him a dismissive little smile.

'I'll see you later,' she murmured to Benson. 'Don't be too long.'

Eager little thing, Dare thought, his fist clenched beneath the tablecloth.

He watched her leave the room, the chandelier above the table lovingly catching the highlights in her hair, before he turned his gaze on the old man.

Benson raised a brow in question and Dare saw just how tired he looked. Whatever news he had just received on the phone it hadn't been good. Not that he felt sorry for the old fool. He'd made his bed years ago and he could lie in it.

'I'm glad you came a day earlier,' Benson said, and Dare was quite sure he wasn't glad at all. 'It has given us a chance to air some grievances.'

Dare hadn't even scratched the surface. 'I won't have my mother hurt.'

'I get that. And I want you to know it's not my intention to hurt her again.'

Dare didn't say anything, just waited for him to continue.

When his grandfather sighed heavily Dare almost felt sorry for him. Almost. 'Your mother is coming for lunch tomorrow. I take it that you're staying.'

'Will the lovely redhead be there?'

His grandfather frowned at his disparaging reference to his mistress. 'Carly is a very nice young woman, Dare, she—'

'Spare me your platitudes. I'm sure she's wonderful.'

'She is. And…yes, she'll be at lunch tomorrow. Is that a problem?'

'Not for me.'

Benson nodded. 'Then I hope you will also accept my hospitality and stay the night.'

'I hadn't planned to.' What he'd planned was to find a hotel room and get some distance from the claustrophobic element of this enormous place, check the Dow Jones, catch up on work, but… His eyes drifted unconsciously to the door Carly Evans had just disappeared through. Practically it made more sense to be on site.

'I'll stay,' he said gruffly.

'Good.' Benson stood up. 'Then, if you'll excuse me, I'll see you in the morning. Oh, and, Dare…' the old man stopped beside his chair '…I understand your concerns. I made grievous mistakes thirty-three years ago. Mistakes I want to rectify.'

'Why now?'

'I have my reasons, reasons I'll share with you when we have more time. For now just know that

I'm not going to let my foolish pride stand in the way again.'

'Just remember that I'll be watching you every step of the way,' Dare said softly. 'And if you do anything to my mother to upset her, I'll ruin you.'

CHAPTER THREE

'YOU KNEW HE'D think that?' Carly paused in the act of placing her stethoscope's bell over the brachial artery in Benson's upper arm.

The Baron had the grace to look contrite. 'Not until I saw the way he was looking at you after my phone call, and then...it was sort of flattering.'

'Flattering?' Carly inflated the cuff. 'Flattering that your grandson thinks I'm your mistress?'

One thirty over eighty. Better.

She tore off the Velcro cuff more forcefully than she intended. 'Only a man would think that,' she griped. 'But he thinks I'm a gold-digger as well.'

'He's a virile male, Carly, and you're a beautiful young woman. His masculinity was dented, that's all.'

'Dented?'

'That you would choose an old codger like me over a young buck like him.'

Carly sighed. 'And men think women are hard to understand. I don't even *know* him!'

'Doesn't matter.' He grimaced. 'How's the blood pressure?'

'Still too high. You know, you don't need this extra stress right now.'

'Probably not.'

'Definitely not.'

But Carly knew what had made him bring it into his life. The operation he was due to undertake was dangerous. At his age it could be fatal. He was putting his affairs in order, although for the life of her she didn't understand how someone could be estranged from their own child for over thirty years!

Her parents would rather cut off an arm than be estranged from her and they still hadn't recovered from her sister's death.

Carly being away this past year was the longest she had ever gone without seeing them and she missed them as much as they missed her. She couldn't imagine not ever seeing them again.

A lump formed in her throat at the thought that none of them would ever see her sister again. It wasn't her fault and yet...

Don't go there, she advised herself. *Focus on your patient.*

'You know, Dare probably would have thought it

even if he knew you were a doctor,' Benson said. 'Beckett thought it as well at first.'

Men, Carly thought. Perhaps she'd give up on them altogether! She didn't know which grandson she disliked more. Dare, probably.

'Perhaps you should just tell them both of your condition,' she suggested. 'Then they'll know why I'm really here.'

'I told Beckett tonight,' he said, moving to the bed. 'But I want to at least spend the weekend with Rachel and Dare before they find out how serious my situation is.'

Carly pulled the covers up over his legs and smoothed them out. 'I don't think Dare will care,' she said cautiously.

'The boy had it hard growing up. I'm only just realising how hard.'

Carly kept quiet. She didn't know the Baron well enough to be in the inner circle of his confidences but she could see that he needed to talk. She handed him his pre-op meds and a glass of water. He swallowed them in one and sighed. 'I really don't blame Dare for hating me.'

'But you'd rather he didn't.'

He smiled up at her. 'No, I'd rather he didn't.'

Carly returned his smile. She was a doctor. Doctors were trained to have good listening ears, although her mother had once claimed that she had always been a good listener as long as her temper wasn't piqued.

She put her stethoscope and sphygmomanometer back in her workbag, snapping the latch closed. 'Just so you know,' she said lightly, 'I'm not playing up to Dare's suspicions about me. I won't be a pawn in this power struggle between you.'

Benson had the grace to look sheepish. 'I know, my dear, and I'm sorry to have put you in such a position tonight. He's angry with me and you got caught in his crosshairs. Both my grandsons could use a good talking-to. Would you mind passing me my phone on your way...?' He touched his forehead and Carly saw a flash of pain cross his weathered features.

'Benson?' She went to him, bending down to see if his pupils were dilated. 'Do you have a headache?'

'No, no... I just have a little business issue to sort out.'

Carly glowered at him. 'You're supposed to be resting.'

'I can rest when I'm dead,' he retorted. 'Especially when someone is meddling with the company my father created.'

'Meddling?' Carly frowned. 'What do you mean?'

'I've lost three pieces of key business lately because there are whispers in the market that someone is going to make a bid for my company.'

Carly frowned. 'Are the two issues linked?'

'I believe so, yes.'

'That sounds a bit underhanded,' she said, 'and not something you should be concerning yourself with right now.'

'I have to if I want BG to survive.'

'Who do you think is responsible?'

'I have my suspicions, but I'm hamstrung in finding out.'

'Dare,' Carly murmured half to herself. 'You think it's him?'

'I was hoping not but after tonight...' He stared past her and Carly felt a well of anger rise up at Dare James all over again.

'But I doubt it's him,' Benson continued. 'Not that I'll rule out the possibility until I've spoken with him in private. Who knows? Maybe he wants to buy BG and sell it off piece by piece. I can't half blame him if he does.'

'Can he afford to do that?' As far as Carly knew

BG Textiles was one of the oldest and most successful companies in England.

'He can afford it ten times over.' Benson made a noise in his throat. 'He's more successful than I ever was.'

'But that's awful if he plans to do that,' Carly exclaimed. 'You don't deserve that.'

Benson gave her a weary look. 'I don't know if he does, but…it's partly my fault if you believe today's psychology. I worked too hard, especially after Pearl's death. I ignored both Rachel and her brother in their formative years.' He sighed. 'I lost my daughter as a consequence, and my son grew up lazy and entitled who spawned a son in his image.'

He coughed into his hand and Carly handed him a glass of water. 'Listen to me. An old man's lamenting. That's another terrible thing about old age. Apart from being that much closer to death you become full of remorse. You see things you never saw before and value things you hadn't even considered. When I was young I thought winning and success were all important. I had Pearl minding the home front and I didn't even know I was missing out on anything until she was gone. Dare, from what I can tell, lives the same way.'

'He's married!' Carly felt so shocked by the thought her heart stopped beating.

'No, no. As far as I know he's single.'

And now it was beating too fast. She had to stop dwelling on that horrible man. 'Well, I can't imagine a woman putting up with him,' she declared with feeling.

'Oh, they put up with him all right. They're banging down his door to get to him.'

'Aesthetically he's very pleasing,' Carly conceded grudgingly, 'but his personality could use some work.'

Benson chuckled. 'Maybe he just needs the love of a good woman.'

Carly glanced up sharply at his tone. 'Don't look at me when you say that,' she cautioned.

'Can you blame me?' He shifted against his pillows and Carly fluffed them. 'He already likes you and you'll make some man very happy one day, my dear.'

Carly felt a lump form in her throat and cleared it away. 'That's very nice of you to say but I'm probably more messed up than your grandson. And you couldn't be more wrong about him liking me. Now go to sleep. I'll see you in the morning.'

Just before she left, the Baron cleared his throat. 'Carly, there's one more thing.'

'Yes?'

'I was hoping you would join us for lunch tomorrow.'

'With Rachel?' Carly said, surprised.

'Yes. It might actually help keep the table balanced.'

What he meant, Carly suspected, was that he might need the moral support. After experiencing the full impact of Darc's calculated put-downs Carly wasn't surprised. Not that she couldn't handle men like Dare James. She'd learnt her lesson well at Daniel's cradle.

'I'd be happy to join you,' she said, and she was. Perhaps Benson would take the opportunity to tell them about his illness—and her real role in his life—and she would hate to miss seeing the shock on his grandson's horrible face.

'Thank you, Carly. You're a true angel.'

Carly gave him a pointed look. 'Call me that again and I'll have Mrs Carlisle serve you tofu for breakfast, lunch, and dinner.'

He chuckled. 'Pearl had your spirit.'

He heaved a sigh and didn't say any more. He didn't have to. He was a worried man who wanted to make amends. It quite broke Carly's heart to see it.

So much so that the following morning, while she tried to jog off her lack of sleep the previous night, she decided that no matter what happened at lunch she would remain completely civil to Dare.

She might not like the man at all, but then she didn't have to. He would be gone at the end of the day and, as she only had two weeks left at Rothmeyer House herself, the chances of seeing him again were slim to none.

Thinking about that reminded her of the email she'd received from her temping agency and had yet to respond to. The truth was she was a little tired of temping, but what would she do instead?

It was one year, three months and four days since they had lost Liv and she knew her parents wanted her home.

But was she ready for that? Ready to run into Daniel? Ready to face the memory of Liv's trusting face as she had held Carly's hand through every oncologist meeting?

The crunch of gravel under her feet soothed her troubled thoughts and she slowed up as the house came into sight. Maybe there was something to this exercise gig, after all, she mused, feeling better. Or was it that she was now anticipating her morning coffee instead?

A small smile lightened her face. Before becoming a doctor she had imagined they were all the epitome of healthiness but really...everyone had their vices and coffee was hers.

Using the bottom of her singlet top to wipe the sweat from her brow, Carly climbed the stone steps that led to the rear balcony and outdoor breakfast table. It was too early for Benson to be up but she still needed to go over the day's menu plan with Mrs Carlisle and—

'Keeping your assets in shape, I see.'

That deep, modulated voice gave Carly a start, the mocking words threatening her earlier resolve to treat this man with distant courtesy and nothing more.

He was once again wearing his faded jeans that surely fitted just a little too snugly, but he'd paired them with a dark grey shirt worn out and rolled at the sleeves, and of course those boots again. The outfit should have looked too casual but on him it looked somehow right, drawing the eye to his wide shoulders and long legs, and Carly hated that her heart skipped a beat at the sight of him.

He gave her a lazy smile as if to say that he knew the effect he was having on her, but little did he know that blatant displays of masculinity had never impressed her overly much. She much preferred someone who displayed gentleness over toughness.

'Good morning, Mr James.' She continued up the steps as if her heart weren't jumping around inside her chest. 'I can recommend a stroll in the east garden this time of the morning. It has a lovely French feel about it.'

'I'm not one for feeling gardens, Miss Evans. French or otherwise.'

Annoyed at the twist he put on her words, Carly kept her back to him as she uncapped the water bottle she had left on the outdoor breakfast table before her run.

'I hope you slept well,' she finally said as he stopped beside her.

'Do you?'

Carly's eyes snapped to his as he leant against one of the teak chairs. 'Let's not start this again.'

'Start what?' he asked innocently.

'The cat-and-mouse game you played last night.' She eyed him balefully. 'I do so hope you enjoyed yourself.'

'Not half as much as I wanted to,' he said, gazing at her through heavily lidded eyes.

Carly was trying very hard to remain calm when he reached for her water bottle and plucked it from her suddenly nerveless fingers. Keeping eye contact, he took a healthy swallow before handing it back. 'Thanks.'

With narrow-eyed calm Carly set the bottle on the table. No way could she drink from it now and by his grin he had expected that reaction from her. Fuming that he should think her so predictable, she snatched the bottle back up and guzzled most of it down.

Unfortunately his deep, amused laugh made her spill some of it and she angrily swiped her mouth with the back of her hand.

'You missed some on your, ah, singlet,' he advised her helpfully.

'If you're looking for your grandfather he doesn't get up before eight-thirty,' she advised waspishly.

'I wasn't.'

'Then if you're heading out for a stroll, please don't let me detain you.'

'I'm not.'

'Then what do you want?' she snapped, raising

her chin and wishing she hadn't when his eyes dropped to her mouth.

Her breath felt trapped in her lungs as her body responded to his sensual gaze with a mind of its own and she stood in appalled silence like a bystander observing a horror car smash.

She couldn't want him. It just wasn't possible and yet all the signs were there… She knew because she'd read about them. She'd just never experienced them before, not without being touched first, and never as strongly as this.

Carly swallowed, thankful that he couldn't possibly know what was going on inside her head, her body. She took a backward step away from him, reminding herself that his interest was no doubt a falsehood designed to give him some advantage over her. After all, he did think she was sleeping with his grandfather!

'I want lots of things,' he said pleasantly, 'but chiefly I'd like to send you packing.'

Carly squared her shoulders. He would not get the better of her this morning. 'Did you wake up on the wrong side of the bed, Mr James?' she said, walking past him.

Dare grabbed her wrist. 'Money-grabbing little tramps should not be left to take advantage of doddery old fools.'

'Really?' Carly glanced down at her wrist as if she couldn't care less that he was holding it. 'For your information your grandfather is not doddery at all. He's completely in charge of his faculties and if he wants to make a fool of himself I'd say that's his business, not yours. In fact, given your attitude, I don't know why you care. Unless it's self-interest.'

His gaze sharpened. 'You think I want you, is that it?'

Carly noticed the sting of colour that ran along the edge of his high cheekbones as his grip on her wrist tightened. He might want her to think he was completely in control but he was very far from it. Not that she cared. She was glad to be able to annoy him the way he did her.

'I meant,' she replied with relish as she peeled his fingers away from her skin, 'Rothmeyer House.'

Dare saw the light of victory in her eyes and could have cursed himself for revealing just how much he wanted this woman. Last night he'd brooded well into the early hours of the morning, imagining her with his grandfather. And since he'd already had his hands on her—albeit innocently—it was more than easy to picture her naked. Picture her breasts, high and round, falling into his hands as he cupped them and brought them to his lips, picture her thighs parting, the silky triangle of red-gold hair guarding her femininity from his gaze.

He had a violent urge to strip her running shorts down her long legs to find out if he was correct about her colouring, to press her up against the cement column behind her and wrap those long silky legs around his hips right before he pumped himself into her.

The image was so visceral he was already at full mast and he knew if she looked down she'd see it.

God, how he disliked this woman. Disliked her cool sensuality and greedy little heart. Disliked the fact that he wanted her to choose him over his grandfather.

What the...?

The wayward thought did nothing to tamp down the primal aggression running like a live wire inside him. He wasn't the possessive type. Not where women were concerned. In fact he couldn't think of anything worse than becoming so enamoured of a woman that he thought about her outside the bedroom, but this woman was like a nagging itch he couldn't scratch. Which was most likely the attraction. She was forbidden fruit.

Knowing it was a mistake but doing it anyway, Dare stepped into her personal space, forcing her to tilt her head back to look up at him. 'I don't need Rothmeyer House or any other of my grandfather's effects,' he snarled, 'but, mark my words, you won't get them either.'

She inhaled a sharp breath, the sound shooting along his nerve endings.

'Fortunately that won't be up to you,' she said, breathing fire. 'And if your grandfather has any sense he—'

Dare grabbed her by the shoulders, effectively cutting off her words. 'He'll what?' he rasped. 'Disown me?'

Carly's eyes widened in surprise before she could school her features. 'Take your hands off me,' she ordered with icy precision.

A feral smile appeared on Dare's face, raising goose bumps along her skin. 'You don't look the worse for wear after last night. Sorry. Did I put my grandfather off his game?'

Carly held herself rigid. 'I said—'

'I noticed you have separate rooms, which tells me the old man can't want you that much.'

Carly sucked in a sharp breath, his words hurting, even though they were incongruous. 'Spying, Mr James?' she mocked.

'Call me Dare.'

'No.'

'Feisty.' His thumbs stroked her collarbones. 'Does my grandfather like that?'

Carly stiffened. 'Doesn't it bother you that you're so preoccupied with your grandfather's sex life?'

His gaze fell to her mouth. 'Maybe I'm preoccupied with yours.'

Ignore him, she told herself. *He's like a tomcat with a half-dead mouse. He wants you to react.*

'Nothing to say, Red?'

Oh, she had plenty to say. 'I'm not going to give you the pleasure,' she said archly.

'Is that right?' he drawled. 'Then maybe I should give you some.'

His hands moved to cup her face, holding her gently despite the hardness of his gaze. Carly couldn't move. If testosterone had a scent it would smell like Dare James, she thought mindlessly.

Dare's thumbs slowly, but inexorably, forced her gaze up to his.

'Aren't you tired of all that aging flesh over yours?' he husked. 'Wouldn't you like to remember what it's like with someone young? Someone virile.'

Carly's hands came up to pry at his wrists, holding them instead. 'Sure,' she said coldly, 'let me know if you find someone who fits that description.'

Instead of being angered into letting her go, he laughed softly, moving so close she could feel the soft cotton of his T-shirt against her singlet. To her utter mortification her nipples peaked.

'Doesn't the old man like to hold you after sex?' he murmured.

Carly didn't know any man who liked to hold her after sex. Not that a grand total of two lovers could be considered vast enough experience. Nor would she tell him that the reason she slept so close to the Baron was in case of a medical emergency. 'How do you know it's what *he* wants?' she tossed at him. 'Maybe it's what *I* want.'

His mouth twisted into an amused smile and his nostrils flared. 'I doubt it. You have high maintenance stamped all over your beautiful little face.

But it's clear that the old man isn't satisfying you. I can smell your arousal even now.'

Ignore him, ignore him.

'Fight it all you want,' he continued softly, 'but you can't hide what your body wants.'

Carly's eyes flew open. 'If you don't let me go immediately I'll scream.'

'I don't think so.' His head lowered slowly towards hers. 'If you were going to scream you would have done it already.' His lips grazed her lower jaw. 'But you don't want to scream, do you, Carly? You want me to kiss you.' His fingers flexed around her jaw. 'To touch you.'

'You think you have me all figured out, don't you?' Carly said, tugging uselessly at his hands.

'Not quite.' His eyes glittered like twin blue flames as they held hers. 'But this should answer a few questions.'

Then he shocked the life out of her and claimed her mouth with his.

Carly froze. She hadn't really believed he would kiss her, but now that he was she didn't know what to do.

Don't do anything, she told herself. *If you don't do anything he'll stop and be completely humiliated. He'll be...he'll be put off.*

She held herself rigidly in his arms as his masterful lips crushed hers, dominating her with angry insolence. She told herself she just had to withstand the pressure, the heat of him, for a moment more. She just had to hold out and he'd change the kiss. He'd…he'd soften his lips and nibble at hers instead of dominating them.

Carly made a small sound in the back of her throat. She could feel the control he exerted over himself in the bunched muscles of his arms, the hard press of his thighs. She never would have thought that physical power in a man was arousing but—

'Oh…' She let out a small breath as his tongue ran along the seam of her lips.

'Yes, that's it, Red. Open up for me,' he commanded gruffly. 'Let me in.'

Carly swayed. *Don't react, don't—* She sighed as Dare slid his hands into her hair and tugged on the band that held her ponytail in place, pulling it free.

The feel of her hair swinging loosely around her shoulders was an added stimulant to the gentle bite of his teeth as he took her lower lip into his mouth and sucked lightly.

Carly heard another soft sound, realised it was

from her, and heard an answering one from him. Then she was opening for him, kissing him back with a hunger she didn't recognise.

He made a victorious groan in the back of his throat but she didn't care because his tongue was in her mouth, his lips claiming hers with long practised strokes that had her melting against him.

She'd simply never been kissed like this before. Never been kissed with such skill and mastery, never felt a man's lips consume hers with such deep hungry pulls at her flesh, and she was powerless to do anything but give into him, her body arching closer to his to ease the ache that had risen up inside her. Nothing else mattered but assuaging that ache and she clung to his shoulders, her fingers tangling in the overlong hair at the nape of his neck. It was thicker than hers, slightly curly, but she couldn't really take it in with his mouth devouring hers so intensely.

His hands moulded her torso, running over her back and then finally cupping her bottom and lifting her into him.

His hungry groan reverberated throughout every cell in her body and his sinful mouth took everything she had to offer and demanded more.

And Carly gave it without thinking, her legs giving out completely.

Dare held her tighter, his mouth forcing her head back on her shoulders, his hand rising to cup her breast, searching out the tip. Carly strained against him. Strained for the pleasure of that first contact...

With a feral sound Dare wrenched his mouth from hers and thrust her away from him, his breathing hard and fast. He stared at her as if what had just happened were her fault.

'No,' he scorned with a shaky laugh. 'Just no.'

Almost savagely he swung away from her and stormed inside the French doors, thankfully leaving her to pull herself together without him watching.

When she finally caught her breath, Carly didn't know who she was most angry with. Dare for grabbing her and kissing her or her for responding.

Flustered and furious, she stormed off towards the kitchen to speak with Mrs Carlisle about the lunch menu. She had a job to do, she reminded herself, and standing around arguing and kissing Dare James wouldn't get it done.

CHAPTER FOUR

'NO, NINA, DON'T worry about forwarding the investor profiles to my handheld, have them delivered to my apartment. I'll be back in London by...' Dare checked his watch. If he left straight after lunch he should make it back by... 'Six, six-thirty.' If he opened up the throttle maybe even five.

Shoving his phone back in his pocket, Dare leaned against the balcony railing and took in the view. Green lawns for as far as the eye could see bordered by manicured hedges and a glassy pond set close to the house. A healthy woodland stretched out beyond the house and behind that a church spire pierced the clear blue sky. No, Benson wasn't doing it tough, he thought cynically.

Unfortunately Dare had needed to tend to some issues at his office all morning so he hadn't had a chance to corner Benson before his mother had arrived.

Then it had been too late. She'd been enveloped

back into her home almost as if she had never left. But she had left, or rather she was forced to leave, and Dare sometimes wondered why she had put up with his father for so many years once it became clear that he wasn't the man she had thought him to be.

Love, he supposed, with a twist to his lips. It didn't always come with hearts and flowers. Sometimes it came with pain and desertion over and over and over.

And to think his mother had come from this genteel society; it was difficult for him to grapple with when he thought about how hard his mother had had it over the years. His pride in her grew even more when he thought about how easily she could have sold herself out and returned to the lap of luxury. But she wasn't that kind of person. She hadn't had it easy just because she could.

His gut clenched.

There was no way the delectable Carly Evans would be duping his mother out of her inheritance if she decided she wanted it. And he hoped she realised by now that he was not a man to cross.

Of course, if his mother did decide she wanted nothing more to do with Rothmeyer House then the little gold-digger could have it and good luck to her. He supposed in her own way she was earning her money and he could hardly blame his grandfather for wanting to keep her. Hell, after that kiss this morning—

Dare stopped his thoughts dead in their tracks.

After that kiss this morning nothing. Why he'd even given into temptation was still eating away at him. It was something his fool father would have done. Gone after a magic moment and to hell with the consequences. And Dare knew Carly hadn't told his grandfather about it because the old man hadn't tried to take him out.

In some way he wished he had because the thought that he'd come on to his own grandfather's mistress made his stomach turn. Especially when he didn't even like her. In fact the only reason he'd even touched her was because she'd damned well goaded him into it.

Yeah, just like Jake Ryan forced you to steal a car when you were fifteen to take a joy-ride that could have ended a lot worse than a lecture from the local sheriff.

Dare sighed. Bottom line he'd wanted to kiss her and so what if it had driven him almost to the point of no return? His emotions were all over the place right now. Unusual, yes, but not unmanageable and certainly not worth thinking about. In a matter of hours she'd be history—at least for him—and he'd consign any memory of her to the bin. Where it belonged.

Hearing voices on the terrace below, he glanced over the wrought-iron railing. His mother was holding a bunch of flowers his grandfather had just given her.

Nice touch, he complimented cynically. His mother loved flowers.

Another voice joined theirs and Carly stepped into his view looking fresh and dazzling in white trousers and a striped T-shirt.

Scowling, he stepped back inside, changed into fresh jeans, a T-shirt and boots. It wasn't exactly garden-party attire, but then he hadn't brought garden-party clothing in the duffle that fitted beneath the seat of his bike. Nor was he in a garden-party frame of mind. And he certainly wasn't here to impress anyone.

He cast his helmet a pained glance. Two hours and he'd be on the open roads again.

'Walk to the village?' Carly repeated, not sure she'd heard right.

She had been counting the seconds until this

torturous lunch would be over and now the Baron wanted her to extend it. And extend it with Dare of all people!

Oh, she knew why he had asked. He wanted some private time with Rachel without his odious grandson breathing down his neck and she couldn't say she blamed him. Sure, Dare hadn't been as hostile as he had been the previous evening, but he hadn't exactly been nice either. But take him on a walk to the village? That was definitely going above and beyond the call of duty. She was here to take care of Benson's *physical* health, not his *emotional* health.

'He'll be bored.'

'I'm game.'

Both she and Dare spoke at the same time and the older two at the table chuckled at them.

Carly's eyes cut to Dare's irritating blue ones, even more vibrant in the matching knit shirt.

He couldn't be serious. Why would he say that when it was clear to anyone watching that he wanted to monitor what went on between his mother and grandfather?

'It's quite a walk,' Carly muttered, hoping her intentions to put him off weren't too obvious.

She had liked Rachel on sight, finding Dare's at-

tractive mother warm and down to earth, her tiny
stature belying a woman with a core of steel. She
also had a core of gentleness and evidently had a
very close relationship with her son.

At first, Carly had wondered if Dare's postur-
ing about protecting his mother hadn't come from
some self-interested space, but she knew immediately she was wrong when she saw them together.
These two people had a connection that reminded
her of the love she shared with her own parents,
and she'd felt a pang of homesickness as she'd
taken her seat at the alfresco dining table.

'I'm young.' Dare smiled at her with only the
slightest trace of mockery in his eyes. 'And fit.
I'm sure I can make it.'

He had been polite to her all lunch and quite a
few times Carly had longed to lash out at him and
show his mother just how rude her son could be
when she wasn't around to see it.

Especially when Gregory had scurried up to
Dare and jumped up at him until Dare had reached
down and placed the little mutt on his lap. As far
as she was concerned the only reason the two of
them got on so well was because they recognised
each other as twin spirits of evil.

'He's really not that scary,' Dare had commented with an arched brow as he'd petted him.

Carly had offered a brief, forced smile, not wanting to find him the least bit amusing. As far as she was concerned he and the adoring dog deserved each other because it had been Gregory's fault she had nearly been run over by the man in the first place.

'A walk sounds lovely,' Rachel agreed, 'and I'm sure Dare won't be bored at all.'

Carly kept a smile on her face as she caught the Baron's pleading look. The man certainly knew how to tug at her heartstrings, that was for sure. And perhaps she could agree to escort Dare into the village and then kick him in the shins once they'd rounded the side of the house.

'Okay, fine,' she groused.

'Don't be too enthusiastic, Red. I might think you like me.'

She'd show him how much she liked him, she thought, right around the next corner.

Smiling pointedly at Benson, she took hold of his wrist. 'I'm sure you and Rachel have a lot of information to exchange.' And he'd better use this time to inform her of his illness or Carly would risk being fired and do it for him!

Satisfied that his pulse was fine, she stood up but not before she caught sight of Dare's narrowed eyes on her hand. She supposed to an outsider her casual touches could be construed as affection, but still… It was a big leap to go from affection to sleeping with someone and it certainly didn't excuse his rudeness towards her, or his grandfather.

Dare had been surprised Carly had not continued to try and wheedle out of their little walk to the village. He'd been surprised even more to find himself accepting the old man's suggestion even before he'd received his mother's not-so-subtle kick in the ankle beneath the table. She wanted time alone with her father. So, okay, he'd give it to her and accompany the little gold-digger into the village.

The little gold-digger who had played his mother like a finely tuned harp at lunch with her polite and surprisingly insightful views on current affairs and international issues. He'd even found himself agreeing with her at one point, but then he supposed if one aimed to become a trophy wife one needed to be able to converse with a variety of intelligent people. Perhaps Miss Carly Evans was just wilier than many of the women of her ilk.

'Okay, this is as far as we go,' she said coldly, stopping suddenly as soon as they were out of sight of the terrace.

Dare glanced at the ten-foot manicured hedges leading to what looked like a maze, and a set of well-kept clinker brick stables off to the left. 'Small village,' he offered.

'Don't be smart,' she snapped, giving him a look that could wipe ten percent off the Dow Jones in seconds. 'We're not going to the village.'

'And what will I tell old Benson when I return and he asks how I found it?'

'They've only thrown us together because they want time alone, you know?'

'I know that,' Dare drawled. 'I'm not an idiot.'

She gave him a look that said she disagreed and shrugged. 'So go polish your bike or something.'

Dare grinned. 'I think you like my bike. Go on, admit it.'

'That death trap?' Carly scoffed. 'Do you know how many emergency-department patients are injured on motorcycles every day?'

He pulled a face. 'I don't think I want to know.'

'Exactly,' Carly said. 'Next time take the bus.'

Dare laughed and she gave him a withering look.

When she made to continue past him he blocked her path. 'And where do you think you're going?'

'To the village.' Her little chin tilted up so high he wanted to nip it with his teeth. Nip it and continue down the long, slender column of her throat until he reached her collarbones and continued on to her sweetly rounded breasts.

'Great.' He cleared the gruffness from his throat and urged his body to settle down. This woman might affect him like no other but she was without morals and God only knew what else—panties, perhaps? 'Come on,' he growled. 'You don't want me telling Benson you're being stubborn.'

'I'm not stubborn.'

Dare took her elbow and laughed softly as she pulled it out of his grasp. 'As a mule.'

'I don't think you would tell him,' she challenged. 'I don't think you'd dare.'

'Try me.' His expression darkened. 'It might make him realise what a disloyal little gold-digger you are.'

'You were the one who kissed me,' she said, outraged colour winging into her cheeks.

'You kissed me back,' he pointed out, wanting to do nothing more than curl his hand around the nape of her neck and remind them both how good it had been. When she glared at him without responding he raised an eyebrow. 'You get points for not trying to deny it.'

'Why bother?' she tossed at him. 'Men like you do what you want anyway. You make your own rules.'

Something in her tone made his gaze sharpen. Rather than look like a woman on the make, she looked suddenly wistful and lost and innocently beautiful, like a woman he wanted to take to his bed and never let go.

And stupid thoughts like that were what had driven his father to follow one rainbow after another.

Scowling, he made an elaborate gesture in the direction of the village.

'Shall we?' he said tersely.

She looked as if she was about to tell him to go jump on his head but then she stuck her nose in the air and stalked off ahead of him.

Dare smiled grimly and set off after her.

They hadn't gone very far when Dare put his hand out in front of her body to stop her.

Startled, Carly threw him an annoyed look until he put his finger to his lips to keep her quiet and pointed into the bracken. A deer and two fawns were grazing on a patch of grass, their ears twitching. Dare could feel the heat of the sun on his shoulders, the soft breeze on his face, and was pleased to sense that Carly was as aware of the delicacy of the moment as he was. A bird called overhead and the deer all raised their heads.

He heard Carly's sharp intake of breath as the doe made eye contact. A moment later her nose twitched and she alerted her fawns before dancing off into the trees.

Dare smiled. He loved the outdoors and since starting his business ten years ago he hadn't had much time to commune with nature as he had done as a boy.

'Oh, my, that was beautiful,' Carly murmured.

'It reminds me of home.'

'Really?' She gazed up at him, wonder turning her gaze soft. 'How so?'

Dare swallowed. 'I grew up in a small town at the foot of the Smokies. Had plans to become a forest ranger at one point.'

Her eyes grew wide. 'What made you switch from forest ranger to finance whiz?'

'Whiz, huh?'

'Some media person's view, not mine.'

Dare shrugged. 'I was good with numbers. My math teacher saw it. He encouraged me, and I won a scholarship to Harvard.'

She nodded slowly. 'That's pretty impressive.'

'Yeah, I like what I do. I like investing in businesses and seeing what I can do with them. Seeing them come off. But living in cities doesn't leave much time to go round up deer.'

And what was he doing sharing his private thoughts with this woman? If he wasn't careful he'd tell her he sometimes felt lonely in those cities, living in large, empty apartments and never feeling settled.

'No deer in Liverpool.' She laughed. 'Our local wildlife consists of teens hanging out at train stations for all the wrong reasons.'

Disgruntled by how much he was enjoying her company, Dare scowled.

'Do you love him?'

She blinked up at him. 'Sorry?'

'The old man,' he rasped. 'Do you love him?'

A cold light entered her lovely eyes. 'Are we

back to that?' She shook her head as if he had disappointed her in some way and his gut clenched. 'But he isn't "the old man", he's your grandfather.'

'And you're evading the question.'

'Because I don't want to ruin my walk any more than it already is.'

She marched away from him. 'Answer the question, Carly.' His long-legged stride easily matched hers.

'Or what?' She glared up at him. 'You'll make me?'

'Is that what you want?' His eyes bored into hers. 'Is the old man too soft for your liking?'

'Oh!' Carly tried to put distance between them but Dare grabbed her elbow and swung her around.

'You're disgusting!'

'You touch him like a lover and yet you're at least fifty years younger than he is. That's not natural.'

Actually she touched him like a doctor—or a friend, at most—but she knew Dare only saw what he wanted to see.

She shrugged off his touch and felt a pang of disappointment when he released her so easily. Incensed by a need she was hard-pressed to understand given her stance on casual intimacy in general, and men like this one in particular, Carly briefly closed her eyes. 'They say the mighty fall the hardest,' she said with a composure she had to fight hard to maintain. 'I so hope that's true.'

He scowled at her. 'If you're not his lover then what are you? Because I'm not buying the whole "friend of a friend" baloney.'

'Ask your grandfather.'

A beat passed between them before he nodded in agreement. 'I intend to.'

Realising that he might be going to do so now and ruin Benson's time alone with his daughter, Carly reached out and grabbed his forearm.

'The village is just over the next rise. I thought you wanted to see it.' She released him. 'Or was your accompanying me just a ruse to get information out of me?' She wouldn't have put it past him.

'Lead on,' he said hardly.

Both relieved and agitated, Carly continued on in silence but it wasn't the comfortable silence of before. Not even the view of the small village as they descended the slight incline onto the High Street was enough to elevate the tension between them.

Carly smiled at a few of the local folk walking by even though she'd never met them before. Which did make her feel better. In Liverpool most everyone kept to themselves in the city streets, hurrying about their business with grim determination. You hardly ever heard laughter in the streets, like here, where some sort of children's game was going on in the village square.

It was a children's birthday party and the game was dodge ball. By tacit agreement both she and Dare stopped to watch, Dare all brooding male energy with his hands shoved deep into his pockets, his shoulders slightly hunched as if he had the weight of the world on them.

If he did she had no doubt that he would come out the victor. Power and strength radiated from him. If this had been a couple of centuries earlier she had no doubt he would have been some kind of war chief with a thousand men at his back.

'I'm not in love with him.' The words were out before she even realised they were there to be said and the air between them pulled even tighter. 'I'm not in love with anyone.'

His eyes flicked to hers and she berated herself for the foolish comment. 'What I mean is…' she took a deep breath. 'You might want to cut your grandfather some slack.'

His eyes flicked to hers. 'Might I?'

Carly sighed. She would probably get more compassion out of a telephone poll. 'Forget I said anything,' she muttered.

The man was as hard as the sand rock used in the construction of the village buildings. Why she'd even said what she had she didn't know. The Baron's secrets were his own to disclose and it wasn't as if she wanted this man to like her, or think well of her. What would that accomplish?

'Then what is he to you?' he demanded, his keen gaze probing hers as if he were intent on learning all her secrets.

'I'd rather not talk about it.' He would find out soon enough and then it would be Carly's turn to have the last laugh. Until then she'd keep her mouth shut.

'You were the one who brought it up this time.'

'My mistake,' she said loftily over her shoulder, circling the small square as if she couldn't wait to see what was growing inside a potted plant across the way.

Dare shoved his hands into his pockets and watched her go. There was more to what was going on here and she held the key. But what was he missing? And why this constant nagging desire to take her into his arms and slay all her demons for her?

Because she had some; he'd sensed it a few times now. And while she might not love his grandfather, there was something between them. He felt it every time she stroked the old man's hand.

And why did seeing that irritate him so much?

Because you want her for yourself.

And he knew better than most that a life based on wanting was no life at all. Which was why he'd based his on action.

'I'm not in love with him. I'm not in love with anyone.'

Dare shook his head. She was doing a number on his head. But was it calculated, or just dumb luck?

He paced over to her, determined to get the truth from her once and for all. 'I know you're not in love with the old man, but you do care for him, don't you?' he demanded, his voice rough with unchecked emotion.

She heaved a laboured sigh as if he were an annoying insect she'd like to see the back of. Well, it was nothing compared to how he felt about her!

'Yes.'

Dare's gut tightened at the honest emotion behind that single word. What if there really was some genuine affection between this woman and his grandfather? What if she wasn't just after him for his money? It made what had happened between them on the terrace even uglier.

But what if she was only playing on his sympathies now? Trying to get him onside so that he didn't fight her for his grandfather's assets later?

Dare stared at the quaint row of shops lining one side of the square. He wasn't used to second-guessing himself all the time, but he'd been doing just that ever since he'd run into her.

Frustrated with his vacillating thoughts, Dare was almost relieved when a child cried out and a forgotten ball bounced past him. Without thinking too much about it he strode forward to where the kids had all clustered around a young girl who sat clutching her ankle, tears coursing down her face.

'Move back,' he said, going down on his haunches in front of the girl.

'Billie!' A woman's frantic voice made him look up as she jostled forward. 'Sweetie, are you okay? What happened?'

'My ankle hurts.'

'I told you not to play too rough. You have ballet tomorrow night—oh, darling, how badly does it hurt?'

'Why don't I carry her over to those seats?' Dare offered.

'No, you shouldn't move her just yet,' Carly interjected tersely.

Dare frowned at her and the woman's gaze flicked between them both before settling on his.

'Oh, well…' She blushed. 'That would be very helpful, thank you.'

Ignoring Carly's venomous glare, Dare lifted the girl into his arms.

'I think it's broken,' the child wailed as he placed her on a nearby bench.

'You'll be fine,' he assured her.

'Here, let me take a look.' Again Carly threw him a dark look and moved to the child's feet.

The mother shifted nervously, peering at Dare. 'Oh, do you think—?'

'I'm a doctor,' Carly said with a ring of authority. 'I can tell you if it's broken.'

'Oh, well, of course, I…'

Carly ignored the child's mother who, she noted cynically, hadn't been so distressed she had missed the bulge in Dare's biceps as he'd picked her daughter up off the ground.

It was pathetic, really, but she supposed if you liked the rugged type with an edge of arrogance and danger about him then this man would be appealing. Very appealing.

'Hi there.' She shoved thoughts of Dare's male appeal out of her mind and smiled at the worried girl, who must have been about ten years old. 'Billie, is it?'

The girl nodded.

'Okay, Billie, I'm just going to have a feel of your leg and you tell me when it hurts and how much, okay?'

Carly was aware the whole time of Dare's searing gaze on her and it took every ounce of professionalism to ignore it.

After a few minutes she announced that the ankle was probably only sprained, but, given the amount of bones in that area of the body combined with the girl's age, she should probably have it X-rayed. 'And in the meantime keep a bag of ice on it. That way you'll keep the swelling down, which will aid the healing process.'

'Oh, thank you, Doctor.' The mother smiled, but it wasn't at her. It was at Dare. No doubt she was still thinking about those broad shoulders and that scruff he hadn't bothered to shave off his horrible face that morning.

Disgusted with herself, Carly stood up and brushed herself off before finally looking at him, unconsciously setting her chin at a challenging angle. This wasn't the moment of victory she had anticipated and she knew Dare wasn't a stupid man. He'd guess straight away that his grandfather was ill.

'So you're a doctor?'

'Yes,' she said as if it were of no importance at all.

He scowled. 'And pretty pleased about it, by the look of you?'

'Why shouldn't I be?' Carly retorted, frowning into his angry face. 'I worked hard for my degree.'

His mouth tightened. 'I don't care if you got it from a paper bag.' He stared at her hard. 'What I want to know is whether you're tired of working so hard, or if the old man is sick and you're his attending physician.' His blue gaze pierced hers. 'Not that I've met too many doctors who live in.'

Okay, so maybe he wasn't that smart, Carly fumed, incensed that he was so determined to think ill of her.

'Unbelievable.' She shook her head. 'You have no shame, do you?'

'Not much. Which is it?'

'None of your business.' She stalked away from him but of course he followed.

'Are you saying that my grandfather's welfare is none of my business?' he asked silkily.

'I'm saying—' Carly stopped and whirled on him '—go take a hike. Off a high cliff preferably.'

Dare grabbed hold of her arm as she turned to walk off and swung her around to face him. 'What is your problem, lady?'

'I'm looking at it.'

'If you would just apply some logic—would you stand still? I'm the one who has a right to be angry here, not you.'

Carly slapped her hands on her hips. 'Of course you do,' Carly soothed with all the ice from the polar cap. 'And I suppose I should be the grateful little maiden on my knees apologising for making you feel that way?'

The air between them pulled taut.

Dare let out a slow breath. Talking to this woman was like trying to pull up weeds with a pair of tweezers. 'If you're on the straight and narrow, why all the cloak-and-dagger stuff?'

Aware of the small crowd still milling around, Carly kept her voice low. 'As far as I'm concerned there is no cloak-and-dagger stuff. There's you jumping up and down drawing conclusions that belong in a Picasso painting and me caught in the crossfire.'

'Little Miss Innocent, is that it?' His lips twisted. 'Or should I say, *Dr* Innocent?'

If she had been expecting an apology—and she had been—she was sorely disappointed. 'Tell me, Mr James, do you have a low opinion of every woman you meet or is it just me?'

'I have a healthy disrespect for lying,' he ground out.

'I haven't lied to you.'

'You haven't been honest either.'

'Maybe it's just that you're so quick to pass judgment on everyone else's motives you don't ask the right questions.'

'If you think being a doctor somehow elevates you above gold-digger status, sweetheart, I have to tell you I've come across a lot of educated women who look at a rich man with dollar signs in their eyes.'

'Maybe women look at you that way because it's the only positive thing about you!' Carly turned and strode towards the path that led back to Roth-meyer House, disconcerted when he easily kept pace with her. 'I, on the other hand, have more sense.'

'Is that right?'

'Yes, that is right. But what's your excuse? Has a woman broken your heart in the past? Is that why you're being so horrible to me?'

'No woman has ever broken my heart.'

'Because you don't have one?' she asked sweetly.

Dare called for patience. 'Because no woman has ever gotten close enough.'

Her brow rose in surprise. 'And never will, by your tone.'

'Correct.'

'So you really have no excuse for making my life hell.'

'I have plenty.' Mainly that he wasn't going to be taken in by a sharp-tongued little witch only to find out later that he'd been played for a fool.

Still… He took a deep breath watching her disappear along the narrow walking path and around the first bend. He wasn't an unreasonable man. At least he never had been before. He frowned. He couldn't seem to get his thoughts straight where she was concerned and that temper of hers didn't help at all.

Scowling, he set off after her, his long strides eating up the distance to catch her up. If she were a new start-up he was interested in, he mused, he'd gather the facts first and then follow his instincts.

'Hold up,' he called when her bright hair came into view, his lips flat-lining when she ignored him. Oh, she was good at that. She'd pretty much pretended he hadn't existed all through lunch.

'I said hold up,' he growled, grabbing her elbow.

'And I said take a hike off a high cliff,' she panted, her eyes the colour of an incoming storm. 'But we don't always get what we want, do we?'

'Would you just listen for once? I want to clear this up and move on.'

She wrenched her arm out of his hold and moved away from him. 'This ought to be good.'

A muscle flexed in his jaw and he let out a slow breath. If she only knew how much he wanted to wrap his fingers around her slender throat and squeeze when she looked at him like that, she'd never do it again.

'So let me see if I've got this right,' he said

calmly. 'You're saying there's absolutely nothing personal between you and my grandfather?'

He waited a beat, pleased with the reasonableness of his tone, when she started laughing.

'Oh, brother!' She tossed her hands up in the air as if he were a delinquent and right now he felt like one. This woman took his logical brain and turned it into a pretzel.

'You are unbelievable,' she stormed on. 'You can't even see what's right in front of your face.'

He took a step towards her, gratified when she involuntarily stepped back.

Oh, yes, my little beauty, you should be afraid if I find out this is all an act.

'I can see very clearly.'

Something in his tone alerted all Carly's feminine instincts that she was standing on rocky ground with a tornado bearing down fast. 'Really?' She felt suddenly breathless. 'And what do you see?'

Dammit. Carly knew her words were a challenge, one she hadn't meant to issue, and his slow smile said he knew it.

'Look, Mr James—'

'I am looking, Miss—sorry—*Dr* Evans, and I see something I like very much.' He took another step towards her, his eyes falling to the lips she'd just moistened. 'But I'm not telling you anything you don't know, am I? You know how desirable you are. How beautiful.'

The words were harsh, spoken more as an insult, but Carly felt her breathing quicken with pleasure at hearing them. A bird called out from somewhere high in the treetops; another answered. Instinct told her to run, while something much stronger kept her immobile.

Carly shook her head as Dare stalked towards her like a slow-moving lion whose prey was cornered.

'No...' A low-hanging branch brushed the back of her head and she swung around to move it. Before she could turn back Dare plastered his larger body along her back, his arms banded around her middle like a steel trap.

'Oh, yes.' His breath was hot against her neck and Carly's knees went weak. 'Your scent drives me crazy,' he growled, his mouth opening over the skin of her neck, his teeth biting down softly. Carly moaned, the back of her head hitting his shoulder.

His hands rose from her stomach to cup her breasts and a need rose up in Carly like never before. The urge to rub her bottom against him was overwhelming. It was like a fire in her blood, burning her up from the inside out.

Don't do it, don't—

Dare groaned deep in his throat. 'Do that again,' he ordered hungrily. A thrill raced through Carly at the naked need in his voice and she was powerless to resist, gasping with pleasure when he plumped her breasts in his hands and squeezed.

'Turn your head, Carly,' he growled against her ear, his fingers circling ever closer to the tight tips of her breasts. 'Kiss me.'

His voice was gruff and mindlessly Carly reached back, curling one of her arms behind her to cup his head and bring his mouth to hers. When their lips met she whimpered and he rewarded her by tweaking her nipples firmly through her clothing.

If Carly had ever felt anything so exquisite before she couldn't remember it. His mouth, those masterful fingers, that hard body covering hers from behind... Time ceased to exist and everything along with it.

Dare whispered her name and turned her in his arms.

Drugged.

He felt drugged as her tongue stroked along his, her mouth wide in an invitation he didn't need to receive twice. Self-control was a distant memory as Dare crushed her lush breasts against his chest. He felt a momentary relief at the contact but then it wasn't enough and he powered her back against the trunk of the hundred-year-old oak.

Her fingers delved into his hair to hold him closer and his hands pushed beneath her T-shirt, shoving her bra higher so that she was completely exposed to him. He took his fill of those perfect orbs and pink-tipped nipples before lowering his head to take one into his mouth. Her taste, the texture of her skin was like ambrosia and he suckled her deeply, his mouth shifting between first one and then the other.

She gripped him tighter, her nails raking his shirt, her keening cries filling the air and he knew she would be wet for him. He knew that all he had to do was lower her to the ground, tug down her zipper and part her legs and she'd be his. All his.

And he nearly did exactly that before a modicum of sanity brought him back to where they were. On a public pathway in the middle of Rothmeyer Forest. Dare wrenched his mouth from her breasts, his eyes grim as they met glazed green ones. 'I'm not going to take you on the forest floor.'

Take her on the forest floor? Carly blinked a couple of times as if she'd just come out of a movie theatre in the middle of the day. Good God, she'd gone crazy!

She couldn't believe the way she'd opened her mouth wide and stroked her tongue along his, the way she'd wanted to strip the clothes from his body and touch him everywhere.

Realising that her bra was digging into her underarms, Carly yanked it back into place and straightened her T-shirt. 'Believe me, I don't want you to take me anywhere. I don't want you to touch me again. Ever!'

His eyes fell to her aroused breasts, her nipples like hard little diamonds against her clothes. 'I told you I don't like liars.'

'I'm not lying, I'm—' She broke off as his hand reached out and covered her breast, his gaze defying her to resist him. And she wanted to, she wanted to be completely unaffected by his touch, but she could feel the tension in her shoulders as she battled to stop her body from arching into his.

'If you'd been wearing a skirt you'd already be

mine and you know it,' he said, his voice hoarse with unmet need.

'I would have stopped you before then,' Carly said with more bravado than she felt, flicking his hand from her breast.

'Would you?'

Dare looked at her mouth, swollen from where he'd ravished it, her cheeks still pink with a passion he'd invoked. She was beautiful. Perhaps the most beautiful woman he'd ever seen.

He rubbed at his chest. Even now the desire to take her in his arms was so strong he had to turn his back on her to prevent himself from doing it again.

How did he just switch it on and off? Carly wondered, still trembling from the force of the emotions he created in her. If he had a secret she wanted to know what it was because she'd use it to turn her reaction to him off permanently. It was almost as if her brain cells ceased to function when he reached for her.

'You enjoyed that, didn't you?' she accused hotly. 'Humiliating me like that.'

His heavy-lidded gaze met hers. 'On the contrary, I thought I was pleasuring you.'

Smug, condescending...

'I won't deny that you know what to do with your hands.' Her eyes dropped to his lips. 'Your mouth.' She raised her chin. 'But you need to know that there is nothing that would induce me to sleep with a man like you.'

A muscle ticked in his jaw. 'And what kind of man is that?'

'A rude, condescending player who takes what he wants and damn the consequences.'

Dare's brows rose. 'A player?'

'I looked you up online last night,' she said, tossing her hair back over her shoulder. 'And you've had more women than I've had patients!'

He cocked a slow grin. 'Considering I don't know how many patients you've had I can't really comment, but I am flattered you took the time to look me up.'

'Don't be,' she shot back. 'I was only interested in what kind of man would treat his own grandfather so callously. And now I know. A horrible one!'

It wasn't quite the put-down she'd been reaching for but Carly was too incensed to care. Straightening her spine she marched away from him, determined never to see him again.

CHAPTER FIVE

'DID YOU HAVE a nice walk, darling?' His mother smiled at Dare as he found her alone in a small, feminine sunroom at the back of the house. 'You know, I really liked Carly. She seems like an intelligent woman and so attractive, don't you think?'

It wasn't difficult to hear the hope in his mother's voice but he hadn't sought her out so she could wax lyrical about the most frustrating woman he had ever met. 'Don't matchmake, Mother, you know I don't like it.' And it was something she had tried more than once before. 'Mark has the car ready to leave when you are.'

'I was just expressing my opinion, Dare. No need to bite my head off.' She sniffed as if he had done her a great injury. 'I can't help it if Carly seemed entirely down to earth and…unpretentious. Normal, even.'

'Unlike the women I usually date.'

'Do you call it dating?' she asked innocently.

'I thought you young people called it hooking up when it only lasted a period of hours.'

Dare scowled. 'If you wanted grandchildren you should have remarried yourself and had more kids.' He felt like a jerk as soon as he saw her hurt face. He, more than anyone else, knew why she had never risked a relationship again. 'I'm sorry.' He ran a frustrated hand through his hair. 'That was uncalled for. But I don't want to talk about Carly. I want to know what happened with Benson after we left.'

She sighed. 'Why don't you come sit down? This used to be one of my favourite rooms when I was a child.'

By the looks of it, his mother had just finished a cup of tea. God, how he hated tea. 'Sorry. Again. I'm a little...' He raked a hand through his hair and glanced around at the cushioned window seats and low side tables. 'How is it being back here?'

'Lovely, actually. In some ways it's almost as if I'm nineteen again. But you're a little what?'

Her parental radar had evidently picked up on his slight hesitation before but there was no way he was going to tell her that he was a little sexually frustrated. 'Nothing.' He smiled encouragingly. 'So what does Benson want?'

She looked as if she wanted to question him more but then she sighed. 'To reconnect. To get to know you. He's a big admirer of yours.'

Dare's eyes narrowed. 'Already?'

'Yes. He looked you up online.'

He was being checked up on a lot, it seemed. Had Carly and his grandfather looked into his past while in bed together? And why was he back to thinking about that when she'd denied sleeping with him?

No, actually, she had denied loving him—she had neatly avoided the whole topic of how deep her involvement with him was and Dare hadn't even noticed.

He frowned. 'That's it? That's all he said?'

'Well, now that you mention it he did ask if I would like to stay on for a few days.'

'What did you say?'

'I said yes.'

And she had a determined glint in her eye that said she wouldn't be swayed. Dare sighed. 'I need to be in the office Monday morning. I can't—'

'I'm not asking you to stay with me, darling, I know how busy you are. But once the two of us started really talking we realised that there's too much to be said in one day.'

Dare's frown deepened. He needed to talk to Benson himself and the sooner, the better.

'Dare, where are you going?'

'To see Benson.'

His mother sighed. 'Dare, be nice.'

He smiled at her. 'I'm always nice, Ma, you know that.'

After searching the downstairs area, Dare found his grandfather in his room with the lovely Dr Evans hovering over him.

'Dare.' The old man said his name with a touch of asperity. 'I'm glad you stopped by.'

He had known he would, Dare thought cynically, guessing by Carly's taut features that she had no doubt warned him that Dare would be on the warpath. Had she also shared anything else? Like those passionate kisses that had temporarily fried his brain?

Unbidden, his eyes shifted to the king-size bed that was—thankfully—without a wrinkle on it.

'We need to talk.'

'Yes,' Benson agreed.

Carly bent close to the old man's ear and murmured something that made him shake his head.

A wave of possessiveness surged through Dare and he clenched his fists at his sides.

'It's not polite to whisper in front of others, Red,' he said. 'Didn't your mother ever teach you that?'

A blush rose up beneath the surface of her skin and all Dare could think about was heat. *Hot, she'd been hotter than the surface of the sun and sweeter than sugar.*

'I wasn't whispering.'

Benson touched the back of her hand reassuringly. 'I'll be all right.'

She clearly disbelieved that; her eyes chilled as they met Dare's.

'I'll see you later,' she murmured to Benson in a voice that, to Dare's ears, promised untold delights.

Benson watched appreciatively as she walked through the adjoining bedroom door before closing it behind her.

'Beautiful, isn't she?'

Dare didn't blink. 'Are you sleeping with her?'

'Direct, as usual,' Benson said dryly. 'I had heard that about you.'

Dare's patience was legendary. Right now it was also non-existent. 'In the States we appreciate directness. So much more effective than kissing someone's butt while waiting to get to the real issue. So, are you?'

Benson sighed. 'Carly is a lovely young woman but you give me far more credit than I deserve. And her far less.'

Dare's jaw clenched. 'A simple yes or no will suffice.'

'No, of course I'm not.'

Dare didn't think he'd felt this sense of relief when the first dot-com company he'd invested all his teenage savings in had been valued as a unicorn in its first year on the markets.

He swiped a hand through his hair. 'So how long do you have left?' Because if Benson wasn't sleeping with Carly Evans then he'd been right all along and the old guy was sick.

To his credit, his grandfather didn't pretend to misinterpret him. 'I don't know. I have a brain tumour they're hoping will shrink before they operate.'

A brain tumour? Hell. He almost felt guilty at his earlier cynicism that the old man was dying.

'And Carly is your oncologist?'

'No, Carly works for an agency I hired because apparently I need twenty-four-hour monitoring due to my diabetes. It's not a combination I recommend,' he said with a flair of black humour.

Dare frowned. 'Why haven't you given my mother this information?' Because he was pretty sure she would have mentioned it if he had.

'It's not public knowledge yet, and I wish for Rachel to want to spend time with me because she wants to, not because I'm gravely ill.'

'You want her forgiveness, you mean.'

'Yes, I want her forgiveness. I behaved badly all those years ago and I'm man enough to admit it.'

'You've had long enough to think about it.'

Benson acknowledged the comment with a rueful grimace. 'You don't pull your punches, do you?'

Dare had lived with a man who used manipulation as a hobby. He wasn't into games as an adult unless they were inside the bedroom and even then they had to be of the pleasurable variety.

'Here's the thing, old man—my mother suffered for years with my father and then for years working three jobs to give me the best start in life. At any time you could have thrown her a bone but you didn't. That makes you unforgivable in my book.'

His grandfather turned grey, but Dare refused

to give a damn. If he wanted forgiveness he was barking up the wrong tree with him.

Finally Benson levered himself out of his chair and pulled an envelope out of his desk drawer.

Handing it to Dare, he sat down to wait. 'Read it,' he urged when Dare just stared at it. The postmark was Australia, where they had lived until Dare was six, at which time they had moved to America.

Knowing he wasn't going to like what was inside, he skimmed his father's handwriting, wincing internally at the shockingly angry letter that would have had the Pope thinking twice before reaching out again.

Then he saw the signature and swore; his startled gaze caught Benson's remote one. 'My mother didn't write this.'

'I know,' Benson said as if in pain. 'Now. I know that now. When I received it twenty-seven years ago I was too proud to question it. And to my shame, I never tried again.' Silence filled the room as Dare stared at the nasty letter.

'And now you're dying and want to put everything right.'

'It's not exactly like that. Three months ago, before I knew my breathing issues were more serious than old age, I saw a photograph in a doctor's surgery. It was some society event in New York and I recognised Rachel straight away. I don't expect you to understand but after seeing her face again…nothing else mattered.'

Dare didn't say anything while he worked through what he'd just discovered. He couldn't imagine how he would respond if he had been in the same situation. Maybe he'd have done the same thing…

'Does my mother know about this letter?'

Benson shook his head. 'I haven't shown her yet.'

'Don't,' Dare decided. 'My father spun so many stories when I was younger I spent most of my youth believing he was a secret-service operative. He used to confide in me and tell me my mother didn't understand and it wasn't until his death that I realised he was just a low-level conman with stars in his eyes.' Dare sighed and handed the letter back. 'And fortunately for you my mother won't need to see this to forgive you.'

'Unlike you.'

'Yeah, unlike me.' Though right now he couldn't say how he felt.

His grandfather sighed. 'A chip off the old block.'

Dare's eyes narrowed dangerously. 'That's the second time you've accused me of being like my father.'

'Actually, I was thinking that you reminded me of myself.' He pulled a face. 'Bitterness burrows deep, Dare, like a tick, and eats away at you slowly, just like a parasite.'

'I have a great life. Nothing to be bitter about.'

'Yes, you've done well for yourself. It interests me that your company is a brokerage firm.'

'More hedge fund,' Dare corrected. 'I raise capital nowadays rather than trade stocks.'

'Capital you can use to buy companies to disband, perhaps?'

Dare shrugged. 'If the company warrants it. Not all companies can be turned around.'

'What about BG Textiles?'

'What about it?'

'We're experiencing some trouble.'

'So I've heard.'

'Heard, or helped create?'

Dare's eyes narrowed. 'What are you implying?'

Benson sighed. 'If I might borrow some of your directness, someone is stalking my company. Is it you?'

Dare laughed. 'Why would I want your company?'

'Perhaps to seek vengeance for the past.'

'If you were any younger, I'd deck you.'

'It would be a nice addition to your portfolio,' Benson persisted. 'And you did expand into the UK this year.'

'I opened an office in the UK because of opportunity, not vengeance. In fact I'd forgotten I even had European relatives until you contacted my mother. Whoever is after BG Textiles, it isn't me.'

Benson took a moment before nodding. 'I believe you.'

'I don't lie.'

'I get that. And to be honest I doubted you were the type who would work behind the scenes to bring the share price down, but I had to ask.'

Which was why his illness wasn't public knowledge, Dare guessed. If it were the share price of BG Textiles wouldn't just fall, it would crash. 'I hope you have some other ideas to follow up.'

'I have some, yes.'

And Dare had no doubt the wily old goat would attempt to get to the bottom of it when he should be resting in preparation for his operation. Not that it was any of Dare's business. If the old man wanted to kill himself sooner rather than later that was his concern.

'I'm sorry, Dare. If I had realised Rachel had reverted to Pearl's maiden name and that you were—'

'Stop there, Benson.' His grandfather's soft words struck like a sharp blade in Dare's chest. 'Shoulda, coulda, woulda—isn't that the expression?' he said stiffly.

Benson's shoulders dropped. 'Yes.'

A knock at the door broke the tension between them and Dare turned, half expecting to see Carly standing in the doorway.

It wasn't. It was the butler asking what time Benson would like Mrs Carlisle to serve dinner.

Once the elderly butler left Benson turned back to Dare. 'Will you stay another night with us, Dare?'

Dare looked at his grandfather's sagging shoulders. The stuffing seemed to have come out of him and he saw lines of strain on his face. He didn't want to stay, he really didn't, but the old man was getting to him, despite his best attempts not to let him.

Someone else was getting to him as well and she'd no doubt be coming down to dinner.

Dinner here, dinner in London… He needed to eat, didn't he? 'I'll stay,' he found himself saying impulsively.

But first he'd head out on his bike and get some fresh air.

And if there was a lightness to his step as he headed back to his room to put on his leathers, it was only because he was finally satisfied that Benson's intentions in communicating with his mother again were born from a genuine desire to make up for the past. It had nothing to do with the fact that his grandfather wasn't sleeping with the delectable Carly Evans. Nothing at all.

CHAPTER SIX

CARLY FELT A sense of relief as she checked her appearance in the mirror before heading down to dinner. She had heard Benson leave his room a few minutes earlier and had almost contemplated excusing herself to eat in her room because of a headache.

Then she'd remembered hearing Dare's death trap roar down the driveway so she knew he'd gone—without saying goodbye, *thank goodness*—so there was really no need to act like a coward. And she enjoyed dinner in the dining room.

Mrs Carlisle usually outdid herself with the evening meal and Carly had never eaten as well as she had since arriving at Rothmeyer House. Probably she never would again. Her beginnings, while not lacking by everyday standards, did not include household staff and a live-in cook! And Mrs Carlisle's cooking would definitely be something she missed when she moved on to her next job.

Something she was still putting off thinking about. She knew she had to go home at some point but...was she ready to return to Liverpool again? In many ways she had loved seeing parts of her country she never had before, but travelling had been Liv's dream and Carly sometimes wondered if she wasn't moving around a lot in an attempt to honour Liv more than herself.

Liv who would never get to travel, never get to fall in love... Carly's heart squeezed and for some reason Dare James's face swam into her consciousness. How on earth she could find a man like him attractive was beyond her.

Yes, he was good-looking...manly...fit...primal... She pulled a face. If you liked that kind of thing. He was also another version of the Daniels of the world. Full of himself, arrogant, rude...and that take-charge mentality? She shuddered.

Yes, it was definitely good that he hadn't bothered to say goodbye or try to apologise. She couldn't have been happier to have things back to normal. And right after dinner she'd set herself up with her computer and make some definite decisions about her life. Maybe she'd move to London and really live it up for once.

Liv would surely laugh at that. Her sister had al-

ways balanced her, pushing Carly out of the house
and out of her studies, or work, to go to movies
or a club, giving her fashion advice and turning
her hair from a layered, carroty mess into the
smoother style she wore it in today.

Feeling the sting of tears at the back of her
throat, Carly twisted said carroty mess into a
quick knot. Liv would have hated Dare James, she
felt sure. She would have said he was overbearing
and obnoxious and… Carly frowned. Actually,
Liv probably would have found him funny and
flirtatious. She definitely would have thought that
his muscles were 'divine'—her favourite expression—and no doubt those rose-coloured glasses
she'd viewed life through would have had her
thinking him a hero always wanting to ride in
and save the day.

Carly shook her head. Some hero coming over
all macho and moving an injured child without
first getting medical clearance. So, it was likely
only a sprain. He hadn't known that, had he?

The man had heartbreak city written all over his
horrible face and it was very lucky he'd gone without saying goodbye because she would have told
him exactly what she thought of him. She would
have told him… A hot flush rose up her neckline

as she remembered the way she had wrapped herself around him in the forest like an anaconda in heat.

God, how embarrassing.

But she wouldn't think about that. The fact was he was gone and she needed to concentrate on her future. On a plan for her future. He could go jump on his white charger and choose some other woman's heart to stomp on. Some other woman to ruin. Her lips twisted into a brittle smile. She'd been in one disastrous relationship already and the old adage held true: once bitten twice shy.

And here she was thinking about him again.

Frustrated, she closed her bedroom door and headed down the hallway. It was just that, okay, she could see the appeal he held with his athletic build, and maybe that take-charge mentality meant that he did things exceptionally well when he did them. Like kiss.

The man knew what to do with his mouth, that was for sure. He'd kissed her as if he'd owned her and she'd loved it. An involuntary shudder raced through her. The truth was, being in Dare James's arms had made her feel incredibly soft and feminine, and, yes, if she was being honest, sexy. He'd made her feel so very sexy.

Her toes curled inside her heels at the thought. No amount of talking to herself late into the night had been able to reassure her that Daniel's constant cheating had been merely a reflection of who he was as a person, instead of who she was as a woman. Somehow she had still felt a small twinge of responsibility for his infidelities because she'd known his libido was a lot higher than hers. He'd told her often enough.

But with Dare…

Carly sighed when she realised where her thoughts were headed again. *He's gone*, she reminded herself briskly. And now she wouldn't be distracted in her care of the Baron, nor would she be constantly on edge, looking over her shoulder for when she might next run into him. He could go throw that swaggering grin and dimpled cheek at some other poor woman and see how she liked it.

A lot, probably. Especially if he kissed her as well. Carly swallowed heavily. If he touched her breasts and did that thing with his fingers—

'Mind if I accompany you down to dinner?'

Whirling around at the sound of his voice, Carly clapped her hand over heart as if that might stop it from flying out of her chest. Goddammit, where was a defib when you needed one?

She sucked in a lungful of air. 'What are you doing, creeping up on me like that?' she fumed. Her face bright red as much from the carnal thoughts she'd been having as the fright she'd just received.

Dare's brow rose questioningly. 'I don't believe I've ever crept anywhere.'

Carly's lips compressed together at his mocking tone. 'Stalking, then.'

He gave a short laugh. 'Not my style either. Maybe this is just a happy coincidence.'

Carly frowned. 'I thought you had left,' she said accusingly.

'Without saying goodbye?' His eyes moved lazily down her body, making her want to squirm. 'Are you really so eager to see the back of me, Red?'

Did he even need to ask? 'You were the one who said you were going,' she pointed out coolly. 'And I heard your raucous death trap take off down the driveway hours ago.'

He shrugged. 'I needed to go for a ride. Clear my thinking.'

God, did that mean he was staying?

He chuckled and she realised he'd read her expression perfectly. 'Don't look so worried, Red. I'm not insulted by your attitude.'

'That's because you have an ego the size of the Himalayas,' Carly griped.

'Maybe I'm just pleased to see you.'

A sharp sensation lodged inside her chest. 'Excuse me, I'm going to dinner.'

'Wait,' Dare said softly, gripping her arm. 'I have a couple of questions I want to ask you first.'

Schooling her features into a bland mask, Carly dislodged his disconcerting touch and looked up at him. 'Like what?'

Dare glanced along the corridor before leaning towards her to speak softly. 'Like how serious is Benson's condition?'

She grimaced. 'So he told you about his illness?'

He gave her a look. 'He told me everything.'

Dare knew she got the full import of his meaning because she blushed prettily.

'And now you're concerned?'

He frowned at her suspicious tone. 'I don't know what I am at this point. But I do want to know what his chances are.'

Carly debated what to tell him and why he wanted to know. Was he going to taunt his grandfather with the information? She really wouldn't put it past him.

'For God's sake, I'm not going to sell the information to the highest bidder, if that's what you're worried about.'

'I'm not worried about that.' She hadn't even considered that side of things. 'What I'm concerned with is what you're going to say to him. His blood pressure is all over the place, which isn't good for him. He needs to rest and not to be overstressed before the operation.'

'And you think I'm going to...what?' He frowned and stepped closer, towering over her. 'Make him feel worse?'

Carly shifted her weight to put some distance between them. 'You were rude enough when you first arrived,' she pointed out

'Hell.' He ran a hand through his hair absently, drawing her attention to the way the caramel tresses drifted through his fingers and offset the strong bones of his face. 'I'm not that cruel. I'm not going to use it against him.'

He sounded genuine, she thought, and it wasn't as if she were giving away secrets anymore.

'Honestly I don't know. If the tumour shrinks enough that they can get it all and his diabetes doesn't complicate things, the prognosis is good that he'll survive the operation. After that it's a bit of a waiting game as to whether or not the cancer has spread. Now, if you'll—'

Dare moved to the left as he sensed Carly about to walk past him, but unfortunately she moved in the same direction and before he knew it her body was plastered up against his. Right where he'd wanted her ever since he'd watched her sexy butt swaying in front of him.

Neither one of them moved for a heartbeat. Two. And then they both took a step back. Her hand went to her hair as if to straighten it and a loose strand caught on the gloss of her lipstick. Dare nearly reached out to fix it himself but shoved his hands into his pockets at the last minute.

Another blush rose up over her creamy cheekbones and her hand shook when she brought it back down to her side. 'This has to stop,' she muttered, frustration etched across her brow. 'I can't explain…'

She stopped abruptly and Dare picked up the thread. 'This thing between us?'

She shook her head in denial. 'There is no thing.'

Dare's smile was slow in coming. 'Oh, there's definitely a thing.'

She let out an annoyed breath and her lips pursed. 'I'm sure it's entirely normal for you to feel this way about a woman but...' as if she'd said too much, her blush deepened, 'I don't like it.'

Nor did he. Not one little bit. And she was wrong about him feeling this way with every woman. He couldn't remember the last time he'd wanted a woman so much his body responded without his brain first giving the go-ahead.

His gaze dropped to her mouth, soft and pink and glossy. If he had met her under different circumstances and trusted her he might take things further. Take her to dinner. To bed. And while his body liked that idea a great deal, instinct told him that walking away was the sanest option. 'Then let's forget it.'

She blinked up at him.

'Just like that?' she blurted out, surprise ripe on her face.

'Absolutely.' Because once Dare made up his mind about something it was done. 'I'm staying one more night,' he said. 'You're here. Why don't we go down to dinner, make nice, then we'll both go to bed—separately, of course—and tomorrow morning I'll drive off into the sunset and it will be as if we never met.'

'Sunrise,' she corrected.

'Sunrise.'

'That sounds…' She squared her shoulders, pulling the silk of her blouse tight across her high breasts. 'That sounds like an excellent idea.'

Yes, it was.

'Shall we?' He directed her to precede him along the hallway. And he'd be fine as long as he didn't put his hands on her.

Which was a bit like telling a three-year-old to keep his fingers out of an open cookie jar, Dare thought ruefully two hours later as the dessert plates were cleared.

For the most part the evening had worked well. Benson was a consummate host and Dare found that he enjoyed hearing about the history of the local village and how it had changed. He especially enjoyed hearing stories about his mother as a child. It surprised him to hear that she had been a rebellious child with a wild streak, but it shouldn't have. It was that side of her, after all, that had seen her fall in love with his conman of a father, and also the side that had seen her knuckle down and go it alone instead of turning to her father for help.

Benson had openly admitted that he hadn't

known how to handle either her, or her after their mother had died and for the first time Dare saw some value in revisiting the past.

But for all his focus on the conversation and enjoyment of the delicious food, nothing could dull his awareness of the slender redhead beside him. Every slide of her leg under the table, every tilt of her wineglass against her lips, every soft laugh as she joined in the conversation ratcheted up his desire to finish what they had started earlier.

It made a mockery of his confident assertion that he could forget the attraction between them *'just like that.'*

And now, with all the barriers to them being intimate effectively removed, Dare was having a hard time convincing himself that his promise to disappear from her life hadn't been just the teensiest bit impetuous.

And what would be wrong with spending a night or two with her? She was an adult, he was an adult…

'Sorry,' she murmured as her hand accidentally brushed his.

'No problem.' He cleared his throat. 'What were you after? The sugar?'

'Yes, thanks.'

Again their hands touched and again he felt an electrical current feather across his skin.

Carly stirred her coffee. Dare shifted in his seat. 'That'll keep you up tonight,' he pointed out softly.

'No, it won't.' She gave him a brief smile. 'You learn pretty quickly as a resident physician to sleep wherever you can, whenever you can, no matter what the circumstances.'

'Sounds hectic.'

'Oh, it is.' Her smoky green eyes were bright with pleasure. 'Emergency departments are busy, chaotic, orderly—which I know seems like a contradiction, but it's not—and really stressful.' Her smile grew. 'Coffee became my best friend during those years.'

'I know what you mean.'

'You do?'

'Sure. You don't put in an all-nighter at a gas station and then race back to campus to sit a three-hour exam after finishing up a paper on the history of economic rationalisation in the Eastern Bloc without a little caffeine hit on the side.'

Carly's eyes sparkled into his. 'Exactly.' Her smile grew. 'But you know the best coffee is the first coffee of the day, right? When it's nice and hot and the acidity just rolls across your tongue.' Her eyes turned heavenwards. 'It's sublime, isn't it?'

'The law of diminishing marginal returns,' he said gruffly.

Her eyebrow cocked. 'Say that again?'

Dare laughed. 'DMR, as I remembered it for the exam. It means that in all productive processes, adding more of one factor of production, while holding all others constant, will at some point yield lower incremental per unit returns.' He chuckled softly at her blank expression. 'In the case of coffee it means the more you drink, the less pleasure you get from it.'

'Oh, now I understand.' She laughed softly and Dare thought in the case of her smiles DMR didn't apply at all.

'What are you two grinning at?'

Grinning?

Dare frowned at his mother's smiling face. He wasn't traditionally a 'grinner.'

'Coffee,' Carly answered, her face carefully blank. 'And whether it keeps you up all night.' She shifted uncomfortably in her seat. 'And on that note I might go up to bed. I hope you don't think I'm rude if I call it a night?'

'Of course not,' Rachel said. 'All that walking today must have made you tired.'

'Yes.'

Carly smiled but it didn't reach her eyes and Dare had no idea what had just happened. One minute they were having a nice time together and the next she was giving him the cold shoulder and brushing him off. Acting as if he didn't exist.

Tension coiled through him tighter than the screws on his Kawasaki. 'Are you sure you're okay?'

'Perfectly fine,' she said briskly.

Dare gave himself a mental shake. If she wanted to go to bed when the night was only half over it was no skin off his nose. He had no hold on what she did. Certainly he had no cause to be irritated by it.

'Sweet dreams, Red,' he said, settling more comfortably in his chair. There was no way he was going to bed at ten o'clock. He wasn't a child.

He lifted the bottle of wine from the bucket. 'More wine, Mother? Benson?'

Carly felt infinitely better after brushing her hair and putting on her pyjamas but, good God, if Dare had touched her leg with his one more time she thought she might have attempted heart-removal surgery with her butter knife.

And not because he had been deliberately awful to her, but because he hadn't! Up until now she hadn't experienced a relaxed Dare and it only made it harder to remember how rude and egotistical he could be.

Her mother had always said that if a man was good to his mother he'd be good to his wife but she didn't want to think of Dare like that. She'd been obtuse in a relationship with a man once before, ergo she could easily fall into the same trap again.

Not happening, she told herself.

Once Dare left in the morning it would be as if they had never met; two strangers who had passed like ships in the night and destined to be nothing more.

A good thing, since she wasn't the casual-sex type and by his own admission he didn't let women get close to him.

And, yes, jumping into bed with Dare James might be utterly thrilling on one level, but what if he was just another mistake waiting to happen? Another bad judgment call? Hadn't she made enough of those already? And not just with men…

Frustrated with the way her thoughts kept veering back to all her failings, she grabbed her computer and placed it on her lap. She logged on and checked her emails. The one from her agency caught her attention and she reopened it.

The job they were offering her was in Kent where a small clinic needed a temporary doctor to fill in while someone went on maternity leave. Would she do it?

Carly bit her lip. A small clinic could be interesting but speaking with Dare tonight had reminded her how much she enjoyed working in a large, thriving hospital. And okay, they were often cesspits for gossip, but it wasn't as if she'd be fool enough to fall for one of the head doctors again.

The question was whether she wanted to reenter that life again. And where? Then there was the question of her flat; the one she'd bought with Liv. She really needed to do something about that.

Oh, Liv, why couldn't I have saved you?

A fist felt as if it had just closed around her heart. What good was a medical degree if you couldn't save people? Anger rose up inside her. Anger at herself. At life. Liv had trusted her and Carly had let her down.

Feeling the threat of tears clog the back of her

throat, Carly fell back against her pillows and took her computer with her. Neither dwelling nor crying had ever brought Liv back to her so Carly didn't let herself do either now.

What she did do was click on a well-known job site and start scrolling down the entries under medical doctors. Don't make a mountain out of a molehill, she told herself.

Lost in thought as she was, she started when there was a thump on her door. She knew immediately who it would be. The Baron was much too circumspect to bang like that, and Rachel would bruise a knuckle if she knocked that hard.

Perhaps if she stayed completely still and pretended to be— 'I didn't tell you to come in,' she informed the man now framed in her open doorway. 'I could have been naked.'

Probably not the best thing to have said. What was wrong with her?

'You knew I'd come up here,' he said arrogantly.

Carly strove to remain calm. 'And why would I know that?'

'Because one minute you're all smiling and happy and the next you look like you'd seen a ghost.'

'You're exaggerating.'

'I don't think so. What's wrong?' he asked, closing the door and moving further into the room.

No way was Carly going to tell him that she'd just been overwhelmed by his presence. That she'd needed some space because he brought up so many painful memories from a past she'd prefer to forget.

That he made her want things she'd rather not want. Like a relationship. A connection. A place to call home.

'Nothing,' she said, trying to ignore the thudding of her heart. 'As you can see, I'm perfectly fine.'

His eyes drifted over her in response to her unintentional invitation. Carly held herself completely still under his steady gaze, conscious that all she was wearing was a cotton singlet and matching boxer shorts adorned with tiny red hearts.

'Perfectly.'

Carly smiled politely at his wry tone. 'Now you can go.'

She watched warily as, instead of doing as she requested, he stopped at the foot of her bed, his hands on his hips.

'Do you always ignore a woman's request?' she asked lightly.

'Was that what it was? It sounded more like an order.'

Unsure of his mood, Carly knew she was strung too tight to deal with him rationally. 'What do you want, Dare?'

His eyes ran over her again. 'Now there's a question.'

Knowing that he was being deliberately provocative, Carly took a deep breath and counted to ten. She had been a resident for three years at one of Liverpool's busiest hospitals having to face down more insolent men than this one. 'I thought you had forgotten all about that,' she challenged.

'Ah, so I did. The only problem is that attraction can be a pesky thing. It doesn't want to stay forgotten.'

'Try harder.' Because this would not end well, she knew it as surely as she knew her own name.

He laughed. 'Easy, Red. I only came to talk.'

Feigning a calm she didn't feel, Carly snatched up her silky robe from the nearby chair and pretended her legs weren't wobbling as she moved to one of the Queen Anne armchairs beside the fireplace.

In winter this would no doubt be a cosy place to hole up in with a good book. Or a lover.

Dare followed her and leant against the mantel-piece.

'I'm curious about something,' he said.

Carly rested back in the chair and curled her legs underneath her. 'Can't you satisfy it some-where else?'

He laughed softly. 'Unfortunately not. Tell me, why does a highly qualified doctor take a lowly nursing position with an elderly man?'

Running was her first thought, hiding her second.

Unsettled by her reflections and the man making her face them, Carly glared up at him.

'First of all,' Carly began frostily, 'nurses are not *lowly* and second of all it's none of your damned business.'

She jumped to her feet and paced away from him.

His brows drew together. 'I didn't mean lowly, as in the profession. I meant as in below your professional capabilities. As I understand it there's a shortage of doctors all over the country.'

'So you're an expert on the medical profession now. Must be nice viewing the world from your lofty heights.'

'I didn't say that.'

'You didn't have to. You just stand there and pass judgment. It's what you do best.'

A muscle flicked in his jaw. 'I only asked a couple of questions.'

Carly took a deep breath. 'I've been at the end of some of your questions before and they're unpleasant to say the least.'

Dare shifted uncomfortably. 'Yeah, about that. I might have made a mistake.'

'One?' She arched a brow, her temper abating at his confession.

'One. Two...' He gave her a quick smile. 'What matters is that, yes, I owe you an apology.'

'Let's have it, then.'

Dare caught her small, slow grin and his deepened. 'You're enjoying yourself.'

'I'm enjoying finally seeing you squirm, yes.'

He tapped his fingers on his chest as if to say, *Who, me?* 'Who said I was squirming? I can admit when I've been wrong.'

'Happens often, does it?'

'No.' Usually he was bang on the money about people. It came from learning from the best shyster around.

'But it did happen this time. And I apologise

for jumping to conclusions about your relationship with my grandfather.'

He watched her throat bob as she swallowed.

'It's fine. I might even have jumped to the same conclusions myself if our positions had been reversed.'

Dare gave a mock frown. 'You mean you would have thought *I* was sleeping with my grandfather?'

Carly's spontaneous burst of laughter made him grin.

'Okay, maybe not,' she conceded.

God, he wanted to kiss her. He'd lied when he'd said he'd stopped by only to talk. He'd stopped by because he'd wanted to see her. Needed to see her.

'Is that why you're really here?'

'What?'

'To apologise.'

Dare let out a slow breath. 'Maybe you intrigue me, Dr Evans. Maybe I just want to know your story,' he said softly.

She moved to stand behind the antique chair and all Dare could think about was shoving the chair aside and throwing her onto the waiting bed behind her.

'My story is boring.'

'Shouldn't I be the judge of that?'

That was just it. She didn't want him to judge her at all.

'If you must know, I had a very normal childhood, with a sister and two parents, and…and I lived in Liverpool up until a year ago.'

'Don't give away too many details, Red.' He smiled. 'What happened a year ago?'

'Why does something have to have happened?'

He shrugged. 'You must have left for some reason.'

'I wanted to travel.'

'That's it?'

Carly narrowed her eyes. He was starting to sound a lot like Daniel during one of his interrogations. Should she tell him that? Tell him that she had been hurt and she should have known better? Tell him her sister had died and she…? Carly swallowed. No, he didn't need to know about Liv.

'I thought I was in love once,' she admitted. 'We dated, and he…cheated. End of story. Happy now?'

No, he wasn't happy to hear she had been in love with another man. Nor was he happy she had been hurt.

'So you left town because of him?'

Her eyes flashed in annoyance. 'Yes, and no, I…I don't want to talk about it.'

'Because you're still in love with him?'

'That's very personal.' Her eyes flicked away. 'But no, I'm not in love with Daniel.'

Daniel?

Dare hadn't wanted a name. He didn't want to be able to picture the idiot she'd been with. And now he was also wondering why she hadn't looked him in the eye when she'd answered him. Was she lying?

Agitated, he absently smoothed his hand along the mantelpiece, accidentally dislodging her handbag and spilling the contents in the process.

'Damn.' He glanced at the array of feminine-looking items scattered at his feet.

'It's okay.' She laughed, kneeling in front of him. 'I've got it.'

Feeling like a fool, Dare crouched down beside her. He handed over her purse and noticed a long velvet box beneath. Curious, he picked it up. 'May I?'

She glanced at the box and blushed. 'It's the necklace I nearly lost.'

So this was where it was.

Slowly opening the box, Dare stared down at the

expensive little number twinkling up at him. This had certainly set someone back a pretty penny.

'Who gave you this? Your ex?'

She finished stuffing the things in her bag and straightened. 'No. It was…no one important.'

Dare knew an evasive answer when he heard one. His brow rose. 'Does he know that?'

'I'm sorry?'

'Does he know he's not important?'

Carly frowned, taking the box from his hand. 'Why are you using that tone again?'

Dare took a deep breath, wondering how it was that he could control a global corporation without batting an eye and yet one woman always seemed to have him on the back foot. Carly was a genuinely nice person—he knew that now. And not only that. She was smart and beautiful and he wanted her.

'Forget I said anything.'

Carly fidgeted with the box before placing it carefully in her bag. 'The person who gave me the necklace did so because he wanted to go out with me. There's nothing else to it.'

Dare doubted that. No man he knew gave a woman expensive jewellery because he wanted to go out with her. It was either a gift to show his appreciation or a parting one. Still...the guy was obviously history and that was all that mattered.

'You don't have to explain yourself to me,' he assured her.

'Good.' She stepped back from him. 'Because, frankly, I'm done with explaining myself to men. There's nothing more debilitating.'

'I agree,' he said, moving closer to her.

'What...? What...? Dare, what are you doing?'

'Taking you in my arms,' he murmured.

Carly flattened her hands against his chest to ward him off. 'Dare, I don't want this. I don't want *you.*'

Dare kissed her. Softly. Sweetly. Carly's breath hitched in her lungs.

'Yes, you do.'

'No.' She shook her head weakly. 'I don't. I...'

He kissed her again. This time it was more commanding. More urgent.

Carly melted. She didn't mean to, but she did. His touch, his scent, his heat—they all set off a minefield of emotions and sensations inside her that she just couldn't fight.

'Carly...'

Dare groaned her name and Carly clung to his broad shoulders. Maybe sleeping with him just once wouldn't be a mistake, she reasoned. Giving in to this desire between them that made her forget everything around her but him. That made her burn.

But then what? a little voice of sanity asked. *Then he leaves and you're left once again to pick up the pieces? Alone this time.*

Carly moaned in denial even as she kissed him. The voice was right. And yet… And yet… She couldn't seem to say no to him.

'Dare, I—'

A beeping sound cut off her weak attempt at resistance and Carly pulled her mouth from his. 'My beeper.'

'Ignore it.' Dare buried his hands in her hair and brought her mouth back to his.

'No. I can't.' Carly pushed at him again. 'It's Benson. I need to give him his medication.'

Dare groaned, loosening his grip with obvious reluctance, and Carly moved out of the circle of his arms, walking like an automaton to her bedside table to silence the beeper.

Dare's heavy breaths filled the room, but Carly kept her back to him. She knew he was waiting for her but she couldn't do this. She felt frozen.

Frozen by her own unbidden desires and the mistakes she had made in the past.

'I think it's best if you go,' she said quietly.

She felt his hard, heated stare before he crossed to her. When he stopped beside her she was almost afraid to look up at him. Afraid she'd back down and tell him she didn't want him to go at all. That she wanted him to love her.

Oh God, that wasn't what she wanted at all.

'Why?' he asked tightly.

Carly shook her head, deeply held fears governing her words. 'I just don't want this.'

'You did a minute ago,' Dare said, a hardness creeping into his voice. 'I felt it. I felt your response.'

'Physically, yes.' She gripped her hands together. 'You're a virile man—I won't deny that—but that's all it is and…and it's not enough.'

Dare stared at her for long seconds. 'I think you're afraid,' he said.

'Afraid?'

'Afraid of the way I make you feel.'

Carly forced out a laugh as his words hit a little too close to the bone. 'And I think you're arrogant and full of yourself.'

Time slowed as his eyes scanned her face, and it

was all she could do not to crumple and ask him to hold her.

'As long as we're clear,' he said coldly.

Carly tilted her chin up. 'I am. I hope you are too.'

His jaw clenched. 'As crystal,' he snarled, before stalking from the room.

Carly held herself perfectly still until he'd slammed the door behind him. Then she sank onto the bed, buried her head in her hands, and wondered if she hadn't just made the biggest mistake of them all.

CHAPTER SEVEN

'You're awfully quiet tonight, Dare. The exhibition not to your liking?'

Dare glanced at the blonde by his side, who was now studying him and not the artwork in front of her. Lucy was a woman he had met a few years ago in New York and they sometimes caught up when they found themselves in the same city, like now.

Apparently she'd come to London to visit a client and since he was still here he'd said yes to her invitation and here he was in a warehouse-sized loft in Whitechapel where Jack the Ripper had carried out his horrifying work.

By the look of the life-size canvases splattered with paint and what looked like debris from the city's gutters, the artist prancing around the room was channelling Jacky boy's macabre energy. Dare wasn't sure he'd seen art that was so gratuitously self-absorbed.

On top of that the beer was flat and the wine tasted terrible.

'The exhibition's fine.' And why spend time explaining his view when Lucy would likely only agree anyway?

Normally at this point he would suggest they call his driver and head back to her hotel. Normally he would already be anticipating the night ahead.

'Well, something is bothering you,' she murmured.

'Nothing of any importance.'

'Anything I can help you with?'

God, he hoped so. It was the other reason he'd said yes when she'd called. He'd hoped very much that she could alleviate the funk he'd been in since he'd driven away from Rothmeyer House in a cloud of dust a week ago.

Nothing seemed to have been the same since then. By rights he should already be back in the States but his meetings were taking longer than they should and his mother was still at Rothmeyer House.

She'd sounded so happy to be extending her stay and spending time with her father and he was, surprisingly, genuinely happy for her. So happy he had agreed to help Benson find out who was behind the leaking of secrets at BG Textiles.

'What do you think of the artist's use of red in this one?' Lucy asked, hooking her arm through his.

Dare glanced at the enormous canvas in front of him. It looked as if the artist had met a shrewish redhead and decided to decapitate her.

His smile was all teeth. 'I like it. It has a certain…something, don't you think?'

'Hmm, I suppose you could be right,' Lucy purred, tilting her head so her hair fell just so across her shoulders.

Carly Evans could learn a thing or two from Lucy about how to attract a man's attention, he thought sourly. Then he scowled. He was tired of thinking about Carly Evans at the most inopportune times. He'd already decided to walk away from her so why bother?

Unfortunately she had burrowed inside his head like a debilitating tick…and his grandfather had been right: they ate away at you with sharp little teeth.

Perhaps she was on his mind so much because he intended to call Benson the following morning and report his findings about BG Textiles.

His *grim* findings.

It was a conversation Dare wasn't looking forward to. How did you tell an old man who was likely dying that his only other grandchild was selling secrets to a company competitor to fund a crappy investment decision he'd made months ago and couldn't repay? From what Dare had found out about Beckett, his fool cousin probably wasn't even aware of how seriously he was putting the company at risk.

And if the information wasn't what Benson was expecting the old man might keel over on the spot and then Dare would have another thing on his conscience. Should he drive down instead? Tell him in person? If he did that he'd likely run into Carly Evans and he could only imagine the type of greeting she'd give him.

But if something did happen to his grandfather after he heard the news the good doctor would surely blame him for it, regardless.

God, she made him mad.

That disapproving little chin of hers would no doubt go up when he arrived, just as it had the morning he'd left. Not that she'd come down to see him off, but he'd seen her, making sure he left from her balcony window.

And that was fine with him. He'd told himself all along not to touch her and nothing good came from not following sound advice.

Finally sick of trying to convince himself that the wine was drinkable, Dare dumped his glass on a nearby table.

'Ah, Dare, I think that's part of the exhibition,' Lucy said.

Dare glanced back at the tall white column and noticed the small card halfway down the side.

'Now it's also useful,' he said. 'Are you ready to leave?'

Lucy curled into his side. 'Whenever you are, lover.'

Yeah, Carly Evans should definitely be here right now taking notes.

He thought about the ruby necklace in her hand-bag. She'd said no one important had given it to her but the poor shmuck must have been at some point.

But why was he back to thinking about her?

She was history and the lovely Lucy was not.

He smiled at Lucy and fitted his arm around her slender waist, guiding her through the throng of fancy-dressed art lovers. Or art haters, if they liked this showing.

Or was that him being judgmental again?

Him? Judgmental?

After living with a father like his Dare knew things were rarely as they seemed, which was why he was such a good analyst. He usually *reserved* his judgment until all the facts were in.

'Dare? Dare?'

Dare glanced down at Lucy. 'What?'

She gave a small laugh. 'Nothing…you just stopped. I wondered if you wanted something.'

'An exorcist?'

'Sorry?' Her laugh this time was tinged with nerves. She drew her blood-red fingernails down the lapel of his jacket. 'I don't know any of those offhand.'

What had Carly's fingernails been like? He hadn't paid any attention to that detail, too busy taking in other parts of her. The graceful arc of her neck, the gentle swell of her small breasts, those long, long legs.

He looked at Lucy. 'It was a joke.'

'Oh!' she murmured. 'You're in a strange mood tonight.'

'Tell me about it.'

He sidestepped a cluster of yuppies and finally spotted the main door.

Thank God for small mercies.

Short. Her fingernails had been short. He remembered the way they'd felt when she'd stroked the nape of his neck and then—he swore softly.

Lucy looked at him as if he'd suddenly morphed into an alien being.

Making a decision, he directed her outside, surprising Mark in the process, who scrambled to open the passenger door for him. Dare waved him off and placed Lucy inside. He couldn't do it. He couldn't be with one woman while he was still thinking about another.

'A change of plans,' he said apologetically. 'I'll have Mark drop you home—or somewhere else, if you prefer.'

Lucy bestowed him with a benevolent smile. 'What's her name?'

'Whose name?'

'The woman you've been thinking about all night.'

Dare hacked out a laugh. 'It's just work.'

Lucy all but rolled her eyes. 'I've known you for three years now and work has never put a frown on your face before.'

'I've had bad days,' he defended. How could

she know him that well when he struggled to remember her surname?

She shook her head. 'You thrive on bad days. This is something else.' She shrugged. 'A woman was my first guess.'

Dare grunted. It pained him to admit that she was right. 'I'll call you,' he said instead.

She sighed and leaned back against the upholstery. 'I won't hold my breath.'

Dare tapped the roof of the car and Mark shot away from the kerb, leaving Dare to either catch a cab or walk home.

He glanced at the sky and turned towards the river. It couldn't be that far to Eaton Square on foot.

An hour later and Dare was reconsidering his decision. His feet hurt and his hair was plastered to his head from the rain that had come out of nowhere. Grimacing, he gave up the ghost and ducked into a small café that was still open.

'Long black,' he said to the pierced barista behind the counter. He could already feel the buzz of caffeine as the youth prepared it and he knew it would be a lot better than the coffee he'd picked up at that grungy gas station he'd worked at during university.

'Thanks. Keep the change.'

He took his coffee to the window and savoured that first sip.

'But you know the best coffee is the first coffee of the day, right? When it's nice and hot and the acidity just rolls across your tongue. It's sublime, isn't it?'

Yes, it was sublime and finally Dare knew what he had to do.

He wouldn't call Benson and give him the news about Beckett over the phone. He'd ride down to Rothmeyer House first thing tomorrow and deliver the bad news in person. Then he'd—no, he wouldn't ride all that way; it would take too long. Instead he'd take the chopper—except the chopper was in for repairs. Damn. So, okay, back to plan A. He'd take the H2 out first thing in the morning and speak to Benson. See if he wanted some advice, given that he was a week out from his operation. Then he'd talk to Carly.

She'd either be happy to see him, or not, and being a man who played the odds he'd put money on not, but either way he wouldn't have these lingering thoughts of *what if?* circling his brain at the most inopportune times. Like yesterday when he'd had to decide if an alarm clock shaped like a pig that was programmed to fry bacon as well was something that was going to take off in the market or tank.

He blew out a slow breath. She'd wanted him as much as he wanted her even if she claimed otherwise.

And if her beeper hadn't gone off he wouldn't still be wondering what it would be like to make love to Carly Evans, he'd know.

Or would he?

Dammit, all these questions were doing his head in. He was a man who dealt in facts, though right now he was behaving like an old woman in a knitting circle.

Well, time would tell. She'd either be amenable to his visit or not and right now he didn't much care which. If she didn't want him he'd walk away and forget her. If she did…if she did he'd tell her it was senseless to fight it. Sex was sex. Why complicate it by abstaining, or over-thinking things?

Stepping outside the café, he walked to the corner and hailed a cab. He settled back against the leather seat, gave the driver his address and glanced out of the window. He felt like a general who had just made the decision to send his troops into battle, his heart thudding so loudly it drowned out the rain on the cab roof.

Carly pulled herself out of the swimming pool and leant back in the sunshine. The weather had been a little cooler this week but the sky was mostly clear and honeybees still hovered over the last of the summer flowers.

Benson's vital signs were all looking good for his operation and she was hopeful that his prognosis would be positive. Especially since he'd developed a real spring in his step with Rachel staying on. It was nice to see them playing bridge together and strolling around the gardens.

Their successful reunion had made her realise how disillusioned she'd become with her own life. Somewhere along the line she'd grown into a non-trusting person—exactly like Daniel, and that was no way to live.

Which was why she'd called her parents. They'd been so happy when she'd called and even said she sounded more like her old self. It had made her feel teary. Without realising it she'd closed herself off from everyone so effectively she'd had no idea just how worried her parents and friends had been about her.

But things would be different from now on. She'd promised to visit when she finished up with the Baron and she'd decided to take some time to figure things out.

And as for Dare James… She was just happy she'd never have to see him again. Her attraction for him had been a complication she hadn't foreseen and most likely hadn't handled that well.

A frown scrunched her brow. If her beeper hadn't gone off she wouldn't have spent the week wondering what it would be like to make love to him—she was quite sure she'd know.

Because he had been right. She *had* wanted him. And it scared her how quickly she'd succumbed to the feelings he'd ignited inside her. How quickly she'd succumbed to his touch, his scent. Pheromones really were powerful aphrodisiacs when it came down to it.

Her hair drifted down her back as she shook her head. At least she could be happy that she had saved herself the ultimate humiliation by not sleeping with him. But what was it he had said? *'I think you're afraid of the way I make you feel.'*

Carly swallowed. He was right, but what did that matter now? When he'd walked out she had known that he wasn't coming back. Which was what she wanted.

'Oh, cut it out, Gregory,' she hollered as the wretched little dog who had been yapping non-stop for the last two minutes kept at it. 'I'm not in the mood!'

When he didn't stop she turned her head to locate what had agitated him—a butterfly flapping its wings perhaps—and caught sight of the recalcitrant little dog, which had seemed to be pining all week, dash across the lawn and round the side of the house.

Great, he'd managed to manoeuvre out of his new collar, the long leash he'd been tethered to lying uselessly on the lawn. Sighing heavily, Carly debated whether to let him go, but then her conscience got the better of her and she deftly rolled to her feet.

Picking her way gingerly across the pebbled walkway with her bare feet, she cursed the little dog the whole time until the unexpected roar of an engine brought her head up.

Like some avenging conqueror from the future, Dare James came tearing along the main drive, kicking up dust in his wake.

He pulled the bike up to within an inch of the portico steps and slowly swung his leg over the side.

Mouth dry, Carly watched him pull the black helmet from his head and shake out his hair. Her heart stopped, and then restarted again at twice the speed.

Gregory spotted him at the same time and ran to him, long silky hair blowing back as he launched himself at the man.

Carly's heart beat double-time as Dare grabbed the dog and ruffled his fur, his eyes on her the whole time. 'Gregory, my old friend.' A slow smile spread across his face. 'What have you brought me?'

Heat suffused Carly's face as she realised she was standing before him in a new emerald-green bikini she had impetuously bought in the village a few days ago. The sales girl had done a number on her and raved about how the colour made her eyes pop.

'I always thought that dog had no sense,' she said waspishly, struggling to contend with the fact that he was standing in front of her, not least of all her embarrassment in being caught at such a disadvantage. 'Now he's confirmed it.'

Dare had the gall to laugh at her discomfort and a shiver went through her at the determined glint in his eyes. Placing Gregory on the ground, he pulled off his gloves and stuffed them inside his helmet. 'It's nice to see you too, Red.'

'Stop calling me that ridiculous name.' It made her want to throw herself into his arms like that wretched, deliriously happy dog had just done.

'It suits you.'

Carly tossed her hair back, telling herself that the safest course of action was to walk away. 'You know that leather get-up and hunk of metal behind you are attention-seeking devices?'

He gave her a slow grin. 'How have you been, Carly?'

'Perfectly fine.' Carly's brow arched at the seductive tilt of his mouth. *Walk away*, she told herself again. 'What do you want, Dare?' she snapped.

'I need to see Benson.'

It took a moment for his words to penetrate the story Carly had unknowingly begun to fabricate in her head that started with Dare telling her he'd missed her and ended with her in his arms.

Mortified by her own insidious attraction for this man, Carly finally took her own advice and whirled away from him, heading back in the direction that she had come. Benson and Rachel were out visiting friends, but Dare could find that out by knocking at the main door.

Unfortunately she'd barely made it two steps before she stood on something sharp and let out a gasp of pain.

'Dammit!' She lifted her foot up to investigate what she might have stood on and lost her balance and landed on her bottom.

Determined to ignore the man who had closed the distance between them, Carly prodded the ball of her foot and noticed what looked like a dried rose thorn marring her skin.

'Need a doctor?'

'No.'

He laughed softly at her snippy tone, unzipped his jacket, and crouched down beside her. 'This is becoming a habit.'

'Not a good one,' she said tersely.

She felt like a fool sitting on a gravel driveway in a tiny bikini while this man was encased in black leather like some marauding invader. 'I can do it,' she insisted when he went to examine her foot.

'I'm sure you can.' He ignored her and wrapped his hand around her ankle, igniting every one of her raw nerve endings in his wake.

And of course he noted her shiver, his brilliant blue eyes searching out hers.

Carly kept her head down and winced when he gently brushed his thumb over the ball of her foot.

'Hold still,' he murmured before squeezing hard.

'Ouch!' Carly jerked her foot clean out of his hold. She knew she was being a baby but being a doctor didn't mean she was able to cope with pain any better than anyone else. In fact she was the ultimate wuss, if the truth be told.

Dare's soft chuckle washed over her and made her shiver again. He reached for her foot, moistened the pad of his thumb with his tongue and then pressed it against her skin. 'Does that hurt?'

Not trusting herself to speak, Carly shook her head and he lowered her foot to the ground but didn't let go of her ankle.

'It should be fine now,' he said, 'and it's not bleeding.'

Carly knew her cheeks must be flushed because her whole body felt hot as she half sat, half sprawled in front of him, but she couldn't move.

She was also aware of how she must look in her nearly nude state. Her chest heaving and her legs splayed apart.

A deep longing rolled through her and she willed Dare to get up. To release her and pretend the chemistry between them didn't exist.

'Carly?'

His fingers flexed around her ankle and Carly shuddered. 'Benson's not here,' she said hoarsely.

She'd meant to say the words to let him know he had wasted his trip, but as soon as she spoke she knew why she had said them. She wanted him. It didn't make sense but what was the point in denying it to herself?

And by the heated glitter in Dare's eyes he knew it too.

Rocks bit into her bottom and a flight of swallows conversed in a nearby hedge, but all Carly could focus on was the frantic beating of her own heart and Dare's darkening eyes. 'Dare, I—'

She stopped as he planted his hands one either side of her waist and leaned over her. Heat suffused the surface of her skin and she breathed in his scent, her tongue coming out to moisten her lips in readiness—

'Damn,' he swore softly and yanked her to her feet.

Her senses scattered to the wind, Carly blinked up at him until the sound of an approaching car finally penetrated the fog of her brain.

'To be continued...' Dare drawled as Benson's Rolls Royce pulled up beside his bike.

'Dare!'

Dare scratched his jaw. *Of all the rotten luck in the world...*

'Benson. Ma.'

'You didn't call and tell me you were coming,' his mother admonished.

'I wanted to surprise you.'

'Well, you certainly did that. Carly, how was the pool?'

'Fine.'

Dare cast her a sideways look. Her lovely mouth was set in a firm line, her body as stiff as a post. So maybe what had nearly happened would not be continued...

He let out a sigh and looked at Benson. 'I have information for you.' And they might as well get that part of his visit over with and move on to more palatable topics. Maybe he might see if he could entice the good doctor back into the pool…

'Okay.' His grandfather nodded tersely. He seemed incredibly frail and Dare realised he really had been blinkered by anger a week ago to have not picked up on the fact that he was not a well man. Had he really grown that cynical?

'Shall we head to the library?' Benson offered.

Dare cast Carly a quick glance but she wasn't looking at him. He'd wanted to check if her foot was all right but she'd likely say yes, and it had only been a small splinter.

'I'll follow you,' Dare said.

'Benson, I should check your pulse first,' Carly called after him.

'How long will this take, Dare?' Benson asked. 'Not long?'

'Can it wait, my dear?'

Carly gave Benson a frustrated look.

'I'll take care of him,' Dare said and got a flash of disgust from her moss-green eyes for his efforts.

Rachel touched Carly's arm. 'Why don't we have tea in the sunroom? I can show you what I bought at the market.'

Carly hesitated. 'Okay, but…I need to change

first,' she said, skipping up the front steps and disappearing into the house.

'Nice wheels,' Benson noted, gazing at Dare's bike.

Dare grinned. 'She does a hundred kilometres an hour in two point six seconds.'

'If only I were younger,' Benson bemoaned, climbing the steps.

Dare followed him and five minutes later yelled for Roberts to bring Carly as quickly as possible.

Dressed in white jeans and a simple green T-shirt, Carly knelt beside the sofa, her black leather bag at her side.

'What happened?'

'I don't know.' Dare's heart thundered inside his chest. 'We were talking and then he collapsed.'

Carly listened to his heartbeat.

'Was he agitated? Upset?'

'No.'

His grandfather had obviously been expecting news that Beckett was somehow involved in his company's problems and, while disappointed, had seemed to take it in stride. He stabbed a hand through his hair. 'But he wasn't completely happy either.'

'We need to get him to a hospital. In London,' Carly said.

'I'll call triple nine.'

CHAPTER EIGHT

HOURS LATER, CARLY stared tight-lipped at the white double doors leading to the operating theatre. Benson had been in there for four hours now, add that to the two-hour flight and it was going to be tough for a patient of his advanced years to survive.

It left Carly feeling quite emotional because the reclusive old guy had grown on her these past weeks, and she hated to see his time with his daughter cut short.

Carly had done everything she could to ensure that didn't happen and she had to admit her job had been made easier by Dare's calm competence at her side. He'd done everything she'd asked of him without question and even organised the best surgeon in London to be on hand when the helicopter flew in.

At one point she was sure he would have put Benson on the back of his superbike if he'd been able to.

Carly knew he'd done it all for his mother, but he'd been slightly grey when Carly had entered the library back at Rothmeyer House and she wondered if there wasn't some level of caring for his grandfather involved deep down.

Regardless, she was glad Dare was on hand because the press were already hounding the hospital to get a story on what had happened to the figurehead of BG Textiles. Not that there was anything anyone could tell them. It was a waiting game from here on in.

'I don't understand why it has to take so long,' Rachel complained.

Carly glanced at the clock on the wall. 'He should be out soon,' she murmured.

Dare looked into the bottom of his coffee cup. 'Who wants coffee?' he asked grimly.

Carly grimaced. Even she couldn't stomach any more hospital-grade coffee. 'No, thanks.'

'Me either, darling,' his mother said.

'DMR,' Dare said.

Rachel blinked up at him. 'Sorry, Dare, what did you say?'

Carly gave him a wan smile. He returned it.

'Nothing, Ma.'

Rachel heaved another long sigh. 'I'd just like

news,' she said softly, standing to stare out of the window at the building opposite.

Dare went and put his arm around her, swamping her small stature with his height and the width of his broad shoulders.

'I'm taking my mother for a walk,' he directed at Carly. 'Will you be okay here?'

Carly nodded. 'I'll call if I hear anything.'

Dare thanked her and directed his protesting mother out of the door, grateful that Carly had stayed but not sure if she had done so because it was her job or…or what? Because he liked having her there?

Not likely. She owed him nothing and the way he'd gone at her when he'd spotted her in that bikini… He sighed.

'He'll be okay,' his mother reassured him, misinterpreting his heavy mood. Which was a good thing because he wasn't about to spill his guts about his feelings for Carly Evans. Especially when he had no idea what they were.

The call came through that Benson was out of surgery just as Dare led his mother back into the waiting room.

Carly looked up and gave them a small smile.

'The surgeon was just here and Benson survived the operation.'

'Oh, thank heavens.' Rachel held her hand over her heart.

'He's in a medically induced coma now, but Dr Lindeman feels confident that he got the tumour. If Benson makes it through the night he should survive the operation.'

Rachel frowned. 'A medically induced coma? I've never understood that.'

'It happens with most critically ill patients who need artificial ventilation to breathe,' Carly explained. 'It doesn't mean anything dire,' she assured her. 'So don't worry overly much. But he will be hooked up to a number of machines, so don't panic when you first see him.'

'Benson's a hard nut,' Dare said gruffly. 'He'll pull through.'

'I hope so.' Rachel buried her face against her son's chest. Carly turned away. Now she could add a caring Dare to his list of attributes, which didn't make her any more comfortable than before.

In fact, she should probably leave mother and son to it as soon as she'd checked in on Benson. It wasn't as if she had to hang around for any personal reasons, was it?

'Rachel James?' The surgeon stopped in the doorway. 'I can take you to see your father now.'

'Really, I can see him?'

The surgeon nodded, directing Dare's mother down the hallway.

Silence filled the small waiting area once they had left and Dare was acutely aware of Carly on the other side of the room.

'Thank you for everything you did today,' he said gruffly.

'It's what I was paid to do. I just wish I'd checked him over before he spoke with you. I might have been able to prevent his collapse.'

'If anyone is to blame, it's me,' he said tersely.

Her startled eyes flew to his. 'No, it's not—I was the one responsible for him. It was my job.'

There was a brittleness to her tone he couldn't place and it made him want to go to her and wrap his arms around her. Unfortunately the icy cloak she had enveloped herself in since they had arrived ensured that he didn't. 'It's been a long day.' She sighed. 'The operation took a lot longer than I expected.'

Dare frowned. 'Is that good or bad?'

'It's neither one way nor the other. It just is,'

she said. 'The important thing is that the surgeon seemed pleased. That's definitely a good sign.'

'I figure doctors are like real estate agents,' he said wryly. 'They say what they think you want to hear.'

Carly gave a small smile. 'That might be considered a touch unethical.'

Dare shoved his hands in his pockets. 'Thanks for staying… It means a lot to my mother. To me.'

She paused, her eyes full of questions he didn't have any immediate answers to. 'I'm…I've grown fond of Benson these past few weeks. He's…' She cut him a brief look. 'He's not as bad as you think he is.'

Dare didn't think he was that bad at all anymore. In fact he'd grown quite fond of the old goat. 'You still think me an utter bastard, don't you?' he rasped out.

Carly looked up at him in surprise. 'No, I don't think that.' She paused. 'I think…I think…'

She stopped, glanced at the floor.

Dare felt his gut clench. He wanted to hold her. Kiss her. 'Red, I—'

'He's alive,' Rachel said with enthusiasm as she flopped down in the visitor's chair again. She gave them a relieved smile. 'But he looks so frail. When will he wake up?' she directed at Carly. 'The surgeon wouldn't give me a straight answer.'

'Without seeing his report I can't answer that, but he's in the best of care here.'

'I know. Thank you for everything you did on the way here. I'm sure he wouldn't have survived without you.'

Carly's sense of relief was immense and she felt immeasurably lighter for it.

'You look tired, Ma,' Dare said. 'Why don't I take you home to rest?'

'I'm not going home tonight. I'm staying here.'

'Don't be ridiculous—you need sleep, and Carly said they're unlikely to wake him up anytime soon.'

'That doesn't matter. I can still talk to him. He'll know I'm here, won't he, Carly?'

Carly gave Dare a rueful glance before responding. 'There is evidence to suggest that coma patients can still hear,' she said carefully. 'But they may not remember anything when they wake up. That being said, some appear to.'

'Then I'm staying.'

Dare scowled at his mother. 'I'll stay with him. You and Carly need to rest.'

'Huff and puff all you like, Dare. My mind is made up.'

Carly watched mother and son face off with amusement.

'Fine.' He turned to Carly. 'What about you?'

Startled to have those sky-blue eyes directed at her once more, Carly swallowed hard. 'What about me?'

'Do you have a place to stay tonight?'

Carly hadn't even turned her mind to where she was going to stay. 'I'll be fine,' she said briskly.

'Yes or no?' Dare growled.

'I said—'

'That's a no,' he decided. 'So you can stay at my apartment. And I know you have to be hungry as well as tired because you didn't eat anything earlier, so don't argue.'

Carly blinked at him. Was he serious? There was no way she could stay in his home. She'd go to a hotel for the night. Because while she did know a couple of people who lived in London she wasn't close enough to any of them to turn up on their doorstep at nine o'clock at night. 'I'll be fine,' she reiterated firmly.

'Dare has an amazing apartment, Carly, and

plenty of room. You'll be more than comfortable staying with him.'

As soon as Rachel weighed in on Dare's side Carly knew this was a battle she wouldn't win. Rachel, she had learned, was as formidable as her son.

'My mother's hard to resist,' Dare murmured as he held the waiting room door open for her to precede him.

'Let's just say I now know where you get your hard-headedness from,' Carly murmured ruefully.

Dare laughed. 'Now I'm really insulted. There's no way I'm as bad as my mother.'

Carly hid a grin and slipped into Dare's waiting limousine. Fortunately traffic was light, either that or they had avoided the main thoroughfares, because they arrived at Dare's Regency apartment block in no time at all.

Dare greeted the smartly dressed doorman and punched the elevator button.

'Top floor?' she asked, her nerves strung tight at the prospect of spending time alone with him.

'Top two.'

'For one person?' Carly stared at him. 'Or is this where you tell me you have sixteen children?'

'I have about sixteen chickens on a small farm back home, does that count?'

'Not quite.'

Carly's lips quirked as she swept past him into the opulent foyer and living room beyond. 'Oh, my,' she murmured. The room seemed to stretch on for a mile of polished wood floors, coffee-coloured walls with white trim, floor-to-ceiling windows framed by silk curtains, and cream inlaid shelving and bookcases along each wall. 'This is magnificent.'

Dare tossed his keys and wallet into a ceramic bowl that sat beside a vase of flowers on a circular table in the centre of the foyer.

'It serves a purpose.'

'Yes,' Carly mused half to herself. 'In some interior magazine.' She walked through to the other room and was almost too scared to step on the cream rugs with her shoes on. The apartment almost put Rothmeyer House to shame.

'There's nothing out of place here. Not even a remote control on the sofa,' she said, following him through to a beautifully appointed kitchen.

'I have a housekeeper when I'm here,' he said, opening the fridge.

'Where's home?'

'Mostly New York. Sometimes San Francisco. Bridget has left chicken pie and salad. I know it's late but I'm starving.'

'And Bridget is?'

His eyes lifted to hers over the door of the fridge. 'Not the mother of my sixteen children,' he said deadpan. 'She's my housekeeper. My elderly housekeeper.'

'Did I ask?'

'You didn't have to. Your face is very expressive.'

God, she hoped not because if it was he'd know…he'd know…

'You look about as exhausted as I feel,' he said softly.

Carly stared at him and blinked. So okay, he didn't have a clue how much she wanted to go into his arms right now. This was a good thing.

'That bad,' she said, grimacing.

Dare chuckled. 'You're still beautiful, Red. You just look like you flew in an emergency chopper from Cornwall to London about eight hundred hours ago—oh, wait. You did.'

Carly gave him a reluctant smile. 'So did you.' And yet he seemed no worse for wear at all. Still gorgeous and powerful and so potently male.

Not even fossicking around in a refrigerator could deter his appeal—if anything it made it worse. Daniel had always put himself above such duties, claiming that his hands were too precious to risk injuring them. And why did she feel the need to constantly compare the two men? It wasn't as if anything was going to happen between Dare and she.

'Do you want a shower?'

Carly nearly let out a low moan at the thought. She would love a shower but just the thought of getting naked with Dare in the apartment was enough to send her mind into a flap. Then there was the small issue that she had nothing clean to change into. Which more or less defeated the purpose of having one. 'I'm good,' she said stoically.

'You sure?' He set a dish on the counter top. 'I can lend you something of mine to wear if you don't want to put those clothes back on.'

'Yours?'

'I'd offer you something of my mother's but she's shorter than you and I had her suitcases delivered to Rothmeyer House last week.'

'I'm happy to sleep in my clothes.'

'Whatever you want.' His expression said she was mad and that was pretty much how she felt.

But then he shrugged and went back to the fridge. 'It's just that I could have them laundered and ready for you in the morning.'

The fact that he was being so reasonable about the whole thing made her feel silly.

'And I suppose you have a laundry service that runs twenty-four-seven at your fingertips?' she quipped.

'Yeah, as a matter of fact I do.' He smiled. 'It's called Dare-o-mat and it's through that door back there.'

A laugh escaped Carly's lips at his unexpected humour and he gave her that grin that set off his dimple.

She couldn't take a breath as she read the way he looked at her. It was the way he'd looked at her so many times before. Right before he kissed her.

Anticipation coursed through her and then her stomach saved her from doing something she'd later regret by grumbling loudly.

'Or perhaps you'd like to eat first.'

Carly blinked as if that might clear her head. 'No, a shower…a shower would be great. Exceptional even.' At the very least it would give her some space to sort her head out.

'Follow me.'

He led her back through the main room to a spiral staircase she hadn't noticed.

She followed him up and when he stopped outside a door she was looking around so much that she nearly ran into him.

Her breath caught. 'Sorry.'

'No.' He cleared his throat. 'That was my fault.' He stepped away from her. Opened the door. 'You can have this room. Bathroom is through the other door. Leave your clothes on the bed and I'll exchange them for a set of mine.'

Carly gripped her bag tighter. 'Your clothes will be too big for me.'

His gaze was hooded when it meshed with hers. 'I'll find something.'

He gave her a brief nod and then closed the door after him. Carly leant against it and let out a pent-up breath. Coming here had been a bad idea, she thought, closing her eyes; a really bad idea.

Dare stopped at the end of the hallway and tipped his head back against the wall. Bringing her here was a bad idea, a really bad idea.

He liked to think that he'd made the offer for her to stay as a good Samaritan, not to jump her bones, but, hell…how much could one man take?

He pushed open his bedroom door and stood inside his walk-in robe. If he just concentrated on the basics maybe he'd be able to find his self-control and put it to good use.

Because he was not going to be such a jerk as to try and sleep with a woman after his grandfather had nearly died. What kind of callous idiot would do that?

So, sweats or shorts? Which would she prefer? And long or short-sleeved shirt? He didn't—

'For God's sake, man, she's not going to a fashion show,' he growled, yanking sweats and a T-shirt off the shelf. He glanced up and caught sight of himself in the mirror. 'You'll eat and go to bed. Alone. God knows, looking at you right now you'd be lucky to ever get laid again.'

Deciding to take a quick shower himself, he changed, and dropped the folded clothes on her bed. Then he snatched hers up, ignoring her floral scent as it rose to his nose, and the sound of the shower through the door, and went to check on dinner.

When it was almost ready he turned and found her standing in the doorway.

Dare looked at her. As she had warned, his clothes were much too big. His T-shirt drooped off one delicate shoulder and reached past her thighs even though he'd pulled out the smallest one, and the sweats… She must have rolled them at her waist but even so he could tell they hung low on her hips and brushed her heels when she walked.

She'd finished by pulling her hair into a rough topknot as if she was showing him that she hadn't made any special attempt to impress him. So different from the other women he had dated who usually took great pains with their appearance.

His fingers tightened around the wooden spoon he held. 'Hungry?'

Because he was famished. And not for Bridget's famed pie.

'Very.'

And there went that fantasy of having her walk up to him and whisper how much she'd like him to lift her onto the benchtop and rip his sweats down her long legs.

'Sit.' He gestured towards the small breakfast nook, wishing he'd worn denim instead of soft cotton.

'So why medicine?' he asked as he shovelled food into his mouth.

'My grandfather was a doctor and I used to be

fascinated by his little black bag and everything in it when I was young.'

Dare smiled. He could just imagine her with her red hair in pigtails and freckles on her nose. 'Did you have freckles?'

Her eyes met his. 'Because of my red hair?'

'Sure. What else?'

She gave him a pained look. 'Yes, I did. My mother always said they would fade because I had Nordic blood and fortunately she was right.'

'So who was the Viking?'

'My father. And he'd love that description. He thinks he's invincible and not at all like your typical academic.' She grinned. 'But he is.'

Dare stared, transfixed by her avid face as she spoke of her parent. 'So you come from a smart family?'

'I suppose so. My mother is a teacher as well, and...'

She stopped and Dare studied the way she stared at her plate as if she'd just discovered a fly on it. 'And...' he prompted lightly.

'And nothing.'

'You know, Red, talking to you sometimes is like trying to get blood from a stone.'

A hesitant smile tugged her lips upwards and

Dare felt an inexplicable urge to reach across and—oh, hell—before he could control it he caught her chin between his thumb and index finger, leaned across the table, and kissed her lips softly. Good God, that felt good, and all he wanted to do was sink into her softness again.

Slowly, reluctantly, he drew back. She blinked her eyes open and looked at him, her gaze smoky green.

'Why did you do that?'

'You looked sad.'

She bit into her lower lip and worried at it. Dare was quite sure she wasn't aware of the action, or what it did to him.

'I was going to say my sister was a social worker.'

'Was?'

'She died a year ago.'

Dare grabbed hold of Carly's restless fingers on the tabletop. 'I'm sorry, Red. How did she die?'

'A rare form of leukaemia.'

Her gaze flitted away again and he paused. Dare felt his heart go out to her. 'That's gotta be hard,' he said softly. 'You want to talk about it?'

'No. Thanks, I...' Carly rubbed at the space between her brows. The fingers of her other hand flexed around his and she stared at where their hands were joined on the table. 'Everything happened so suddenly. One day Liv was well and healthy and helping kids in need and the next she was gone.' Her throat bobbed as she swallowed. 'The doctors tried but...' She grimaced. 'They couldn't do anything and as much as I searched...' She took a deep breath, her gaze miles away.

'You couldn't save her either,' he said quietly.

Carly looked up as if startled that he had understood her so well. But it wasn't hard. Not when she fascinated him so much.

'No,' she said, the word coming out gruff. 'And now I don't know what to do.' She gave a self-deprecating smile. 'I've thought about giving up on medicine but something stops me. Years of study probably.'

'Why would you give up on medicine?' He frowned. 'Because you feel like you failed your sister?'

'I did fail her,' she said in a pained whisper. 'When she said that she wanted to try some alternative medicines I encouraged her not to. I told her to trust her doctor. I told her that he would know best.' She pulled her hand from his, tucked it into her lap. 'If I hadn't intervened...'

'If you hadn't intervened, what?' Dare asked softly. 'She would have lived?'

'Yes!' Carly exclaimed. 'Maybe...' she added as he continued to look at her.

'Is that what the doctors believe or what *you* believe?'

Carly buried her face in her hands. 'I know it's not logical.'

'Emotion rarely is,' he said wryly. 'But I doubt your sister would want you to give up medicine, Carly. The fact is, not every person can be saved.'

'I know that too. I know...' She unconsciously lowered her hands into the prayer position. 'I miss her so much.'

Dare took her hands in his. Judging by her response, he doubted she had ever opened up about the responsibility she had erroneously taken on with regard to her sister's death.

'Come here.'

When she didn't move Dare stood up and came around to her. 'Dare, I don't—'

Ignoring her, he slowly drew her to her feet and, like a small stream bubbling over smooth rocks, Carly flowed towards him.

'Dare—'

He drew her closer. 'I just want to hold you.'

An odd tightness gripped Carly's chest. 'I don't need anyone to hold me, I'm—'

'Perfectly fine.' He pulled her in against his chest anyway. 'Humour me, hmm? Hell, after listening to that I need a hug.'

Carly felt a wave of tenderness envelop her. He didn't really need a hug, he was only trying to be nice, but, oh, how wonderful it felt to lean against him. To soak up some of his warmth. His strength. His *hardness*.

She breathed in deeply and felt his arms tighten around her like soothing bands. Taking away that lost feeling she'd carried around with her for so long and replacing it with comfort and heat.

She wasn't sure when she felt the change come over her but within a heartbeat comfort and soothing became something else entirely. Carly froze and tried to fight the urge to shift against him to assuage just a little of the ache building inside her.

Dare felt her subtle movements and swallowed heavily. He shouldn't have touched her. Even though he'd only been offering comfort, he'd known that wasn't all he wanted to do. He wanted her so badly he'd had to force himself not to grab her all night and now she was in his arms, her soft breasts pressed against his chest. Her hot breath like a flame against his throat.

Dare stifled a groan. To make a move on her now when she was vulnerable from the events of the day and her memories of the past would put him squarely in that bastard category she'd assigned him to a week ago. Now he had the chance to confirm that, or he could—

'Carly? Carly, baby, don't…just keep still.'

Dare loosened his grip a little when she squirmed again. He half expected her to pull back and when she didn't he looked down into her upturned face.

The lighting wasn't overly bright in the room but it was bright enough that he saw the flush on her cheeks and the darkened pupils, the way her eyes were fixed on his mouth. He felt her muscles tense and his body read the meaning even before his brain had fully engaged with the idea.

Oh, who was he kidding? His brain, his body, his very being was invested in this and he was done trying to pretend that it wasn't.

'Carly.' His voice was deep and gravelly and he felt her tremble in response.

Dare set his hands to her hips. He wanted to

take this slow and easy. He'd dreamt of having her beneath him ever since he'd met her and—

'Dare?'

Her gaze rose from his lips to his eyes and that was all it took to cement their destiny. His mouth swooped to hers, devouring her without any regard for finesse or seduction. He was hungry, ravenous, and she was exactly what he wanted to eat.

She opened wide to him and Dare groaned, one hand buried in her hair to hold her exactly where he wanted her and the other pressing her against his erection.

She made a soft, kittenish sound that drove him wild, and her hands kneaded his shirt, her teeth biting at his lower lip as if she was as hungry as he was.

'If you don't want this, Carly,' he rasped against the delicate shell of her ear, 'then stop me now.'

She gave him one of those exquisite little shivers, her body arching almost involuntarily towards his. 'I want it.' She forked her own hand into his hair and dragged his mouth back to hers. 'I want you to make love to me. I *need* you to make love to me.'

Dare understood exactly what she meant. This feeling between them was a celebration of life and loss and for some reason he needed it just as much as he sensed she did.

Her heartbeat thundered against his, although it could have just been his own, and Dare lifted her up as if she weighed little more than a feather.

'Legs, around my waist,' he croaked, already moving in the direction of his bedroom. His blood was storming through his veins and his mind was consumed with the smell and feel of her, his body throbbing to just throw her down on the floor right now.

'Damn.' He groaned as she squeezed her ankles over his backside. He could feel her hot core through their layers of soft cotton and he gripped the staircase to steady himself.

He'd never had to navigate his spiral stairs with an armload of woman before and he laughed softly as she clung on like a spider monkey, attacking his neck with her sharp little teeth and lathing him with her tongue.

Dare very nearly disgraced himself and then, thank God, the bed was in front of him and he dropped her onto it and yanked the sweats down her long legs.

Slow down, buddy, his mind warned, but Dare was caught in a fever trap of desire he'd never experienced before and the need to make her his beat out his conscience.

He pulled his own clothes off and grabbed her ankles, spreading her wide.

'Condom,' she breathed, bringing him back from the hazy edge of insanity.

'Damn.' He dragged his gaze from the heart of her body to her face and tried to rein himself in. This was too much. Way too much...

He gazed into her eyes that were overbright with a lust that matched his own and he knew he wasn't strong enough to heed the distant warning bell in his head.

Swearing as he hadn't since he was a teenager, he stormed into his bathroom and grabbed condoms. Since he didn't ever bring women back to his sanctuary he didn't have any by the bed. He would now.

Rolling one on, he returned moments later to find Carly leaning up on her elbows, her vivid hair falling to the pale bedclothes behind her. There was a sense of wariness in her eyes and she looked as if she was trying to regulate her breathing.

'Second thoughts?' he asked gruffly, praying to God she said no.

Her eyes flared wide as she took him in, her

gaze hot as it skated down his chest and lingered on his shaft. He knew what she saw. He wasn't a small man by any means and he was so hard the tip was resting against his belly.

His eyes narrowed in on her reaction to the sight of him and if possible he went even harder as her legs shifted restlessly on the mattress, her lips parting as she breathed shallowly.

Goddamn, she was beautiful.

'No.'

Dare's breathing stopped. 'No?' he got out hoarsely.

'Yes, I mean no...' She shifted again as if she was aching for his possession. 'No second thoughts.'

Thank God.

Dare grabbed her ankles again and slid his hands to her knees, only mildly less rough than before as he urged them to part. She was still wearing his T-shirt, her breasts thrusting against the fabric.

'Take the shirt off,' he growled.

His heart felt as if it were trying to work its way out of his chest as she struggled to get the fabric over her head. When she was free of it she tossed it to the side and looked up at him.

Dare's gaze roamed over her pert breasts, her coral-coloured nipples standing to attention, her narrow waist and flared hips. 'Holy, sweet mother of… Tell me you're ready for me, Red.'

'I am. I—'

He glanced down at the dewy entrance to her body and fitted himself against her. She was so wet he slid in easily but he stopped part way, giving her body time to expand around him.

He held himself still, sweat turning his skin slick, until he felt her tight inner walls clench and release and then he thrust forward in one powerful motion, coming over the top of her, his hands on either side of her head.

She groaned when he fully seated himself inside her and, worried that he'd hurt her, he paused again. She whimpered and raised her hips, sliding her inner thighs along the outside of his and shattering his self-control in the process. 'Oh, yeah, Red, grip me tight.'

Dare powered into her, angling his hands beneath her bottom so that he hit the sweet spot that made her gasp and rub herself against him. He knew what she needed and, holding on by a thread, he thrust into her over and over until he felt her body stiffen right before it fluttered and rippled around him, signalling her climax and drawing him in deep; sending him spinning on his own powerful vortex of completion.

Nothing, nothing had ever felt this good. He was sure of it and he only raised his sweat-soaked body from hers when he felt her stir beneath him.

Good, she wasn't dead, was his first thought. Good, he wasn't either, was his second. Or if he was they were dead together and it didn't matter.

'Are you okay?'

'I'm not sure,' she panted, her arms lax above her head. 'I may never move again but if that's normal, then yes, I'm okay.'

Dare chuckled and eased out of her. Nothing about what had just happened was normal but his brain was too stupefied to analyse it. 'I'm sorry...'

'Why?'

'I came at you like an animal.'

'We are animals.'

He gave a soft laugh. 'Only a doctor would say that.'

With strength returning to his limbs, he levered himself off the bed and went to dispose of the condom. When he returned she was sitting up in bed and looked delightfully rumpled. She also looked as comfortable as a cat on a hot tin roof.

Dare didn't know what to think, actually he still wasn't thinking, so he acted on instinct instead, bending to her and cupping her face in his hands. When her lips softened after a momentary resistance he stroked her tongue with his, feeling himself hardening all over again.

She made a little moaning sound and he nudged her backwards onto the bed.

'Dare?'

'Shh…' he murmured. 'Let me love you properly.'

'I'm not—oh!' She stilled as he licked across the tip of her breast, her small nipple tightening in response.

'I didn't get to say hi to these guys,' he said.

Her soft laugh turned into a small whimper as he tongued her and drew her nipple into his mouth, suckling deeply.

'Damn, you taste good, Red.' And he needed to explore her. Explore every inch of her to find out what she liked and what she didn't.

Like this little pressure point in the bend in her elbow that made her gasp when he licked it, and the soft skin at the base of her throat that made her arch upwards, begging him to feast on her breasts again. And, oh, yeah, she really liked that.

'Dare, I don't think we should do this again.' She shoved her hands in his hair as he flicked her nipple with his tongue but instead of pushing him away she held him closer, making sweet little female sounds that had that primal part of him wanting to ditch the foreplay and move right on to the mating.

But he wasn't going to do that this time because he was enjoying himself too much. It was as if no man had ever taken the time to give her pleasure and those sweet little keening sounds were turning him inside out.

God, she was hot. So hot. 'Open your legs for me,' he murmured, nuzzling the undersides of her breasts and working his way south over the smooth skin of her belly.

'Dare.'

He shifted so he lay flat between her soft thighs, his chin resting on the golden red curls hiding her moist heat. 'You know that ex of yours was the biggest loser letting you go, don't you?'

She arched her head back as he parted her with his tongue.

'He never...I didn't...'

'Go down on you? Love you with his mouth? Taste your sweet, womanly essence?'

He punctuated each sentence with light, playful flicks of his skilful tongue, honing her senses to the point where nothing else existed but him. And her. And this.

'Oh, God, I never thought I'd find talking in bed such a turn-on.' She gripped his head in her hands. 'Please, don't stop,' she begged.

Dare chuckled and blew a breath over her femininity. 'Don't stop what?' he teased. 'Talking? Or don't stop this.' He licked her again, more firmly this time.

'That.' She twisted against him. 'Don't stop that. Don't stop anything. It's so sexy.'

'You're the sexy one, Red. Sweet and sexy. Like your scent.'

'Oh! God, I'm going to come.' She made to pull away from him as sensation overwhelmed her but Dare held her hips tight until they shuddered with pleasure as she came against his mouth.

'Dare… Dare…' She chanted his name, reaching for him blindly, her fingernails digging into his shoulders, his hair. 'I need you. Please, take me.'

Not forgetting a condom this time, Dare rolled a rubber down his rigid length and rolled on top of her. This time when he entered her he did so slowly, savouring the exquisite warmth of her body closing around his.

He groaned, determined to make it last, thrusting into her with firm, measured strokes until he couldn't take any more. Until he felt the soft pulsing of her body and that little hitch in her voice that told him she was on the edge. Then, only then, did he completely let himself fall over the cliff with her and down the other side.

What could have been hours, or only minutes, later Dare woke to find Carly sleeping beside him. He gently moved a strand of her hair to the side, gathered her against him and fell back to sleep with a satisfied smile on his face.

CHAPTER NINE

CARLY WOKE SLOWLY to the sound of a ringing phone. She moaned softly as her body ached in places it hadn't before and then she blushed as memory returned full force.

At the sound of Dare's deep voice she scrambled for the sheet and pulled it up over herself. Seconds later Dare walked out of the bathroom with a towel slung low around his lean hips, his chest and arms rippling with lean, hard muscle.

Oh, my God, she thought, *he is a demigod. A bronzed demigod who belongs in the V&A.*

'Benson is awake,' he said, tossing the phone onto the side table.

Okay, so they were going to play this completely normal. Good to know. 'What did the surgeon say?'

'It was my mother and she sounded very optimistic.' Which told Carly nothing at all. Family of critically ill patients always veered towards the bright side in these situations.

'Your clothes are dry,' Dare continued. 'I was planning to visit him. Do you want to come?'

'Of course.' Benson was still her patient—sort of—and even though she wouldn't be his attending physician post-op, she would have hung around to make sure he was all right, regardless.

They were both quiet on the drive to the hospital. On Carly's part she was still sorting through what had happened the previous night. It still stunned her that she had opened up about Liv the way that she had. Not so much that she'd told him, but more that she'd expressed her anger. Her bitter disappointment with herself. And Dare was right: Liv wouldn't want her to give up medicine. Nor would she want her to run and cut everyone off the way that she had. It had all seemed so hopeless a year ago. But in Dare's arms…when he'd held her and soothed her…

Carly swallowed heavily. And the way he'd made love to her.

She released a slow breath, hoping he was so engrossed in returning work emails he wouldn't notice.

At least, she presumed he was returning work emails. For all she knew he could be lining up his next woman.

And when had she become so insecure?

She sighed again. She was not going to blow this out of proportion. It had happened and it had been wonderful. More wonderful than she could have ever imagined. She made a face. She had thought she'd reached orgasm before but apparently she'd been wrong.

But sex—no matter how earth-shattering—was not grounds to start measuring up white picket fences or planting fruit trees that took years to bear produce. She'd learned that lesson the hard way. And it wasn't as if she had fallen in love with him. That would be...

Carly's hand squeezed her throat.

Love? Who mentioned love?

She swallowed. Tried to breathe.

She wasn't in love with him. She wouldn't be that foolishly stupid. That brainless to fall for a man so much more potent than Daniel he might break her completely if she let him.

'That's a lot of sighing going on over there. You okay?'

Startled, Carly glanced at him. 'Fine.'

His smile cocked a little. 'You sure?'

He reached out and entwined his fingers with hers.

Carly's heart kicked against her rib cage. God, the man was lethal.

'Absolutely.' Absently, Carly wondered if she could add acting to her résumé. But this was important. She needed to keep things in perspective. Dare wasn't interested in long-term relationships and neither was she. 'But I was thinking,' she continued, 'that it would be best not to let anyone know what happened last night.'

Dare frowned. 'Because?'

'Well, because I don't want to lose my job with the agency for sleeping with a client's son, if it's all the same to you, and I'm worried that Rachel and Benson might read more into it than they should.'

'Don't go getting your knickers in a twist,' he said easily. 'I was only asking.'

She hadn't realised she'd been holding her breath until his cavalier response, and then she felt silly. 'God, you're arrogant,' she said, her temper directed mainly at herself.

She was doing it again—making mountains where there should have been molehills.

He grinned at her. 'Next time I'm making you a morning coffee whether you think we have time or not.'

Next time? Carly's heart gave another jolt. She let out a breath. What was wrong with her this morning? 'Sorry,' she grumbled. 'I'm worried about Benson.' Which wasn't *untrue*, she thought. She *was* worried about him.

'Forget it.'

Dare rubbed her fingers almost absently.

He'd woken up this morning to his ringing phone and hadn't had time to think about much between then and now. Which meant that he hadn't thought about how he was going to play this thing with Carly in front of Benson and his mother.

And it irked him a little that she had because he was usually on top of these things. And it irked him more that she was right.

If his mother knew he had taken Carly to his bed the previous night she'd be matchmaking within minutes. Actually she probably already was. It was as inevitable as breathing really. She wanted grandkids and short of adopting a set for him she saw potential in every woman he went out with.

Well, almost every woman. Okay, so she hadn't seen potential in any woman he'd dated so far, but that didn't stop her from wanting him to meet someone and fall in love. And Carly was a perfect candidate. Smart, sweet-natured, beautiful, sexy.

Man, was she ever sexy. If his mother knew how compatible they were between the sheets she'd be asking what jeweller he was going to.

Probably Tiffany's. He'd purchase one of those diamond rocks as big as his fist. He smiled as he thought of how his ring would look on her long, slender fingers. Maybe he'd get one a little smaller than his fist, he decided, but it would be as perfect as her smile.

He frowned, then let go of her hand to fiddle with his phone.

His heart felt as if it had relocated into his throat and he took a deep breath.

What the hell had just happened? One minute he was thinking about sex and the next thing he was mentally shopping for rings? Okay, so it had been the best sex he'd ever had, but a ring?

He chuckled, and reached for her hand again. She looked at him questioningly and he kissed the backs of her fingers. Smiled. For a minute there he'd nearly lost his head.

Benson was awake when they got to the room, but barely. He was still heavily sedated. Dare leant against the small window and watched Carly going over the doctor's notes on his chart. His mother also watched her, waiting for her verdict that the other doctors hadn't been feeding her false hope.

'It all looks good.' She smiled at his mother. 'Of course, we won't know the results of the tumour for a couple of days but he's responding really well to the post-op meds.'

'That's a relief.' Dare's mother gripped his grandfather's hand in hers.

Before Carly could say anything more the door opened and his cousin, Beckett, swaggered in unannounced. Dare had never met him before and he remained completely unmoved as the younger man's eyes briefly narrowed in on him.

So far Dare had dug up quite a bit on his privileged cousin and he'd found that if stupidity and sleaziness were a crime Beckett would be in jail for life. Perhaps if good looks were a crime he'd be there even longer because even Dare could see that his cousin had been genetically blessed in that department.

'I came as soon as I heard,' Beckett gushed.

Dare stared at him. He'd like to know who had told him about Benson's condition, but kept silent.

'You must be my aunt Rachel,' Beckett said, as smooth as a snake gliding over sand. 'It's a pleasure to meet you at last.' He took her hand and kissed the back of it before turning to Dare. 'And you, cousin Dare.'

Dare folded his arms and tucked his thumbs beneath his armpits. 'Beckett.'

Beckett acknowledged the rebuff with a small smile and turned to Carly.

'Carly.' He said her name on a sigh and Dare's senses sharpened. 'It's good to see you again.'

'Beckett, how are you?'

'Better for knowing that my grandfather has survived his operation.' He smiled down at her, squeezing her shoulder. 'And for seeing you again. But I am a little miffed at you—' he pouted '—for not letting on about my grandfather's condition.'

'It wasn't my place to mention it,' Carly said, moving away to replace the clipboard at the end of Benson's bed. Which was fortunate for his cousin, Dare brooded, because he'd been about to rip his arm from its socket.

When the clipboard wouldn't catch Dare stepped between the two of them. 'Here, let me help you, Red,' he murmured softly.

Beckett ignored him, his gaze lingering on Carly a little longer. 'And how is he?'

Dare listened while Carly filled his cousin in.

Beckett showed genuine concern for his grandfather, but Dare's hackles were raised. Fortunately his cousin had enough sense to pick up on Dare's cool regard and didn't prolong his visit. Which was a good thing. Dare didn't trust him, and he definitely didn't like the familiar way he had touched Carly.

His lover.

He pushed away from the windowsill. He wanted nothing more than to take Carly away from here and sweep her into his arms again. He wanted to kiss her long and hard and deep and feel her melt against him. Hear her make those breathy little moans he was rapidly becoming addicted to and smell her woman's smell. Taste her again. And if some small part of his logical side found that a bit disturbing, well, he would deal with that later.

He slung his arm around his mother's shoulders and dropped a kiss on her head, asked her how she was. He felt good. Really good. Why deny it?

Carly watched mother and son converse and she knew she'd lied to herself in the car. Somewhere in amongst the arguing and the accusations, the tenderness and the desire, she had fallen in love with him. Completely and stupidly in love with the arrogant, the self-assured Dare James.

The feeling was so different from how she had felt about Daniel that she finally recognised that there was some truth to her father's assessment that she had fallen for Daniel to help her deal with Liv's diagnosis. She hadn't wanted to face that because she'd needed a better reason than that as to why she had let him treat her so badly. It made her feel as if she had a terrible weakness inside herself that would allow any man she became involved with to walk all over her if he pleased.

Like this man.

Carly's breathing bottomed out as a slow panic set in like molasses sliding down the tip of a spoon. Before she knew it she was at the door and pulling it open.

'Carly?'

Schooling her features, she pinned a smile on her face before turning back to the occupants in the room. 'I'm just heading out.' And never coming back. 'Give you all some time together.'

She pulled the door firmly closed and barely registered the nurses' station as she strode past.

'Carly!'

Dare caught up with her just outside the lifts.

Carly stabbed at the button.

'Where are you going?'

Carly stared at the lift doors, willing them to open. 'I need to find a hotel for the night and—'

'What are you talking about?' he asked gruffly. 'You're staying with me.'

She heard the frown in his voice and made the mistake of glancing up at him. 'Dare, I—'

'Unless you're going to say last night was a one-night stand.'

'No, I—'

'That I took advantage of your vulnerable state.'

'I would never say that,' Carly said hotly.

'Good.' He looked altogether too satisfied with himself and Carly's temper spiked. 'Then we're decided.'

'You might be,' Carly snapped, 'but I'm not. And I'm tired of you pushing your way arou—'

'Carly?' He said her name softly, a burning intensity entering his blue eyes as he stared down at her. 'Stay with me.'

His earnest request was such a shock Carly's anger dissipated as quickly as it had arisen. Then she shook her head. Staying would be emotional suicide. 'Why?'

He frowned. 'Because something is going on

here.' He placed his hands on her hips and a shiver raced through her. 'Between us. I know you feel it. Damn, after last night…I'm not ready to let it go.'

'Something?' she asked, holding her breath.

He leant his forehead against hers. 'I don't have a label for it, but—' he exhaled '—I can't explain it except to say that I've never wanted a woman as much as I want you.' He leaned back to look down at her. 'Spend the day with me.'

Carly searched his gaze and felt that same surge of love she'd felt well up inside her when she'd stared at him before. And something else, besides. *Hope?* Was it possible he felt the same as she did but didn't know it yet?

'Don't you have to work?'

He smiled down at her. 'At this rate I'll have meetings banked up until Christmas but I don't care.'

He bent his head and kissed her softly. She moaned against his mouth, rose up onto her toes to kiss him back. The lift door pinged its arrival and they ignored it.

When a couple of the occupants tried to manoeuvre past, Dare shifted them both to the side without breaking their embrace.

Carly released a nervous laugh.

'I want you.' He clasped her face in his hands, his blue eyes intense. 'All of you. Every bit of you.'

Every word was tautly spoken, his broad shoulders stiff with tension, as if he were the one standing on the edge of a cliff top wondering whether to go over. But that was only her, wasn't it?

She looked up at him and said the only thing that she could. 'Yes.'

CHAPTER TEN

DESPITE THE OVERHANGING grey clouds and constant threat of humid rain they had a glorious day. They walked along the Thames, had lunch in a tiny French bistro, and came across that horrendous art exhibition Dare had attended with Lucy. He had nearly groaned when Carly wanted to take a look inside, having the good sense not to mention that he'd already been.

'It looks like the artist really disliked his last girlfriend,' she mused. 'Or boyfriend.'

Dare laughed and asked her what she thought of the white column thing that still looked like a table to him.

After that they talked about everything from politics to Hollywood movies and which was better, *Thor* or *Iron Man*. She waxed lyrical over Chris Hemsworth; he might have mentioned Charlize Theron once or twice.

'Charlize, huh?'

'She's a fine actress,' he explained with a straight face. 'She's won awards.'

'Yes, but I bet it's not her awards you picture when you think of her,' she teased.

No, he didn't, but for some reason with Carly standing in front of him with shafts of sunlight striking her hair he couldn't bring any other woman to mind.

'You think?' he said.

She laughed and Dare grabbed her and dragged her up onto her toes in the middle of a busy street, forked his hands in her hair and kissed her.

After that they headed to his apartment. Made love.

He couldn't get enough of her and if he had enough brain cells left in his head he'd probably be worried about that.

'How can you have black coffee when you have this wicked-looking machine that can probably grow the beans, collect them, and roast them at the same time?' she asked.

She was wearing one of his T-shirts and he'd bet nothing underneath. He loved it when she did that.

'I like top-shelf stuff,' he said, thinking of her.

She perched on the edge of a stool. 'Because you never had it growing up?'

They'd talked a bit about his childhood. Nothing too drastic, just where he'd gone to school, how he'd had to work hard to put himself through college, his first car—a 1990 Mazda RX-7 he'd been so proud of at the time. But things he'd never discussed with anyone before.

'Yeah, I suppose so.' He gave her a quick smile. 'You might not believe this but I was a scrawny kid when I was younger, always coming from the bottom.'

'Oh, I bet you liked that!' She laughed.

He grinned. 'I might have gotten my head punched in a few times when guys tried to push me around about it.'

'What did your dad say? Did he step in and threaten to do the same to them?'

Dare's grin slipped a notch. 'My father wasn't around much.'

'Why not?'

'He was a dreamer.'

'A dreamer?'

Dare nearly laughed. Saying his father was a dreamer was putting it mildly. And part of him wanted to tell her everything. Tell her how he had looked up to his father, believing in him right up until his death, tell her how he had defended his father in the schoolyard, tell her how bitterly disappointed he was to find out that he was just a liar. But the words stuck like a block of cement in his throat.

And why sully the moment by rehashing the past? Especially when she was looking at him the way she was. All big-eyed and soft-mouthed.

'He's not worth talking about,' he said, pouring the coffee.

'Is he still alive?'

'No. He died when I was fifteen. Here,' he announced with a masculine flourish. 'One girlie coffee for your tasting pleasure. Tell me that isn't the best coffee you've ever tasted in your life.'

Carly knew Dare was deliberately changing the subject and she told herself it didn't mean anything.

Giving him a quick smile, she forced herself to sip the warm liquid. It really was good. She blinked up at him, wondering if there was anything he couldn't do well. 'Mmm...' She rolled her lips together, savouring the taste. 'You're right, it is good. But the best...' She took another sip. Licked her lips again.

Dare stared at her mouth. 'Now you've done it,' he said, coming around to her side of the counter.

'Done what?' Carly asked innocently.

'Gone and made something hard,' he growled, lifting her onto the benchtop. 'And seeing as how you're a doctor and all, you might like to take a look. Give me your professional opinion.'

'My professional opinion, huh?' Carly reached down and cupped him in her hand. Dare groaned.

She frowned at him. 'Hmm, my professional opinion is that you really should do something about that.' She tapped her finger to her lips. 'I'm just not sure what.'

Dare lifted his shirt to her waist. 'Here, I have an idea.'

A faint stream of early morning sunlight woke her and once more Carly's internal muscles cramped pleasurably as she moved. This time, however, instead of waking alone she found Dare still with her, sprawled out on his back, one arm flung over his head, the other curled beneath her neck.

Carefully, so she didn't wake him, Carly rose up on her elbow and looked down at him.

He was magnificent. His dark beard growth making his jaw appear even squarer, his dark lashes creating a thick curve on his cheekbones.

Last night he had been both passionate and

gentle. Powerful and tender. And completely insatiable. *She* had been completely insatiable. Waking in the early hours of the morning to find his mouth on her as he drew her from sleep in the most delicious way imaginable.

But it wasn't just the way he made her feel that mesmerised her. It was the man himself. He was so strong, so sure of himself and, yes, controlling, but that was somehow part of his appeal, much as she never thought she'd ever say such a thing!

'What are you looking at?' he rumbled without opening his eyes.

Carly grinned. God, she loved him, and her heart felt as if it were glowing inside her chest.

'You,' she said, leaning down to gently kiss his jaw.

The arm beneath her came around her shoulders and he lazily caressed her spine.

'A little less looking and a lot more action would be preferable,' he advised with drowsy appreciation.

Carly laughed. 'You're insatiable.'

'Hmm.' He gripped the nape of her neck and encouraged her head to bend to his. 'I am where you're concerned.'

Carly stroked his chest. 'We should check how Benson is doing.'

'I already did.'

'You did?'

'I woke up earlier and called the hospital. They're thinking of moving him out of ICU later today.'

'Oh, that's fantastic news.' She smiled at him, drawing slow circles on the sprinkling of hair on his chest. 'That was nice of you to check. I think "the old man" is growing on you,' she teased.

Dare grunted and she hid a smile against his shoulder. He came over all cold and tough, but deep down he wasn't. Deep down he was the man of her dreams.

'Are you accusing me of going soft?' he murmured suggestively.

'Never!'

She squealed as he rolled her onto her back and held her hands above her head. 'Let me up,' she said breathlessly.

His eyes drifted over her naked breasts. 'Make me.'

Carly reviewed her options and her stomach chose that moment to growl loudly.

Dare's eyebrows rose in alarm. 'Okay, I give up.'

Carly laughed at his antics. 'I haven't eaten for hours,' she defended.

'Then I'd better feed you.' He rolled away from her. 'How does an American omelette sound?'

'Great, but what's the difference between an American omelette and our omelettes?'

He dropped a kiss on her mouth. 'We *cook* ours.'

Carly grinned, watching him tug on his jeans, leaving the top button undone, with the casual disregard of a confident male.

A surge of emotion shook her out of her happy delirium as it struck her that maybe she needed to pull back a little.

'Why don't you have a shower while I cook?'

She swallowed heavily and shook off the maudlin thought. Dare wasn't a mistake. How could he be when it felt so good?

'Sounds like a plan.' She smiled.

'Oh, I have plans for you, Red. I'm just building your stamina first.'

'Promises, promises.' Carly laughed and she headed for the shower.

Dare pulled a carton of eggs and a block of cheese from the fridge, a frying pan from the cupboard.

He was humming, he realised, and grinned. He

couldn't remember a time he'd felt this good. This amped. Maybe when he'd seen his risky stock options turn him from a possible contender on the financial markets to a man everyone respected. And maybe when he was speeding along an open road. But never with a woman before.

He glanced at the day outside the window. It wasn't raining so maybe he'd try and get his doc to set aside her reservations and hop on the back of his death trap with him.

He frowned.

His doc?

She wasn't his anything. She was very definitely her own woman and he could only imagine her temper taking hold if he suggested anything else.

He cracked eggs, ground pepper and salt into a bowl, and grinned.

That ex of hers had really done him a favour, he thought, cheating on her. The guy must have been a moron. It was the only explanation Dare could come up with because Carly was magnificent. Everything a man could ever want in a woman.

He stopped stirring. What was he thinking? *That he was going to keep her?*

His heart found its way into his throat. Was that what he wanted?

He stared into space.

Yes, the answer came back, yes, *he did want her*, and that was when he knew that he could no longer avoid the truth. Somehow, some time, he'd fallen in love with the lovely, the beautiful Dr Evans. And he wasn't even worried about it. The fact was he'd never met a woman like her. So open and honest, so genuine and giving. And, man, was she ever giving. Last night—

The buzzer sounded on his intercom and almost bemusedly he pressed the button.

If someone had told him a week ago he'd fall in love with a feisty redhead he would have laughed. Deep down he'd believed love wasn't something he'd ever want or something he would ever need.

'What's up, George?'

'Sir, a Mr Beckett Granger is here to see you.'

Dare frowned and almost told him to tell Beckett to take a hike, to use one of Carly's expressions.

Then he thought better of it. Better to talk to Beckett here than at the hospital.

'Send him up, George.'

And what about Carly? he wondered. Was she falling in love with him too?

He recalled the breathy little sighs she made

when he touched her, the way she moaned his name, the smile she'd given him when he'd woken up this morning that had nearly blinded him. Was that just lust or was it—?

'What the hell are you playing at?'

Distracted as he was, Dare wasn't even aware that he'd opened his front door until a very angry Beckett dressed in a pinstripe suit and smelling like a men's fragrance counter pushed past him into his home.

Dare swore under his breath and caught up with him in two strides but by then he was already in his open-plan living room.

'What do you want, Beckett?'

Beckett swung round. 'Nice digs. Glad someone can afford them.'

Dare stared at him. 'I repeat, what do you want?'

Beckett took his time answering. 'So I tried to log in to my computer this morning only to find that I've been banned from accessing certain parts of the business.'

'I hope you didn't bother Benson with that,' Dare snarled, knowing their grandfather wasn't fit for that kind of discussion just yet.

'I wasn't allowed because his *watchdog* said he

was sleeping. But I figured you'd know all about it. And I'm right, aren't I?'

'We can discuss this later. At my office. If you call my PA she'll make an appointment for you.' And if he ever called his mother a watchdog again, Dare would deck him.

'I don't want to make an appointment. I want an explanation. Now.'

'I'm not prepared to discuss it,' Dare said.

Not until he'd spoken to Benson to see how his grandfather wanted to play things. This wasn't Dare's issue and, while he'd followed Benson's instructions to have BG's second-in-command take over as acting CEO, he wasn't about to further isolate Beckett without first knowing what damage he could do. 'And now you can—'

'Why, Dr Evans,' Beckett simpered as he glanced behind Dare. 'How very…unexpected.'

'Beckett? What are you doing here?'

Having heard voices, Carly had come to investigate and now wished she had taken the time to dress in more than one of Dare's T-shirts because Beckett was openly staring at her legs. And her breasts.

Carly folded her arms across her chest, gazing

from one man to the other, and wondering if she shouldn't make herself scarce.

'It would seem that we have the same taste in women,' Beckett murmured and Carly very definitely thought about making herself scarce.

'Excuse me?' Dare's quiet question was lethal.

Beckett paused before smiling. 'I have dibs.'

Carly frowned. 'Don't be rude, Beckett,' she said sharply, remembering that she still had his necklace in her handbag.

Beckett ignored her in favour of Dare. 'Or is Grandfather just up to his old matchmaking tricks again? He really fell for our doctor here,' he informed Dare. 'I suppose he doesn't care which grandson ends up with her.'

Carly felt herself blush. Beckett was being a complete plonker. 'There was never anything between us, Beckett,' she said coldly.

'Oh Carly.' Beckett thumped his chest with his fist. 'You wound me.'

'Just because you're angry about what's happened at BG Textiles doesn't mean you have to make this personal,' Dare bit out.

Carly smiled. His defence of her warmed her heart.

'Besides,' Dare continued, 'I think we have

more important things to discuss. Like your insider-trading efforts.'

Insider trading?

Carly's eyes flew to Beckett's. If Dare was right, then Beckett could be in a lot of trouble.

Beckett's face took on a mottled hue. 'Don't you dare try to tarnish my name to get the inheritance for yourself,' Beckett spat.

'As you so rightly pointed out when you walked in, I don't need Benson's inheritance. Nor do I need to try and tarnish your name. You're doing a good job of that all by yourself.'

'Sometimes I wish I had been born two centuries ago,' Beckett spat, 'because then I'd call you out for that slur.'

Dare gave him a bored look. 'Don't fret it. You would have lost.'

'You absolute, utter—'

'I suggest you leave without saying another word, cousin,' Dare broke in softly.

'Or what?' Beckett seethed. 'You'll take something else from me? Or hit me, perhaps? Go on, I dare you.'

Dare yawned.

Carly planted her hands on her hips. 'If he

doesn't I might,' she warned. 'There's absolutely no need for any of this, Beckett.'

Beckett turned to her, his expression tenderly forlorn.

'Allow a man to express a little outraged jealousy, *Red*. I did find you first.'

Red!

He had never called her that before.

Carly noticed Dare take a step in Beckett's direction and shot forward. 'Wait.' She held her hand up to Dare and turned to Beckett. 'Don't move and don't say another word,' she instructed. Then she rushed from the room and pulled the velvet box out of her bag, wishing she'd remembered it at the hospital the previous day.

'This is yours,' she said, pushing the velvet box into his hand. Her eyes flashed to Dare as he stood by the front door, unconsciously noting his lethal stillness.

'I gave it to you.' Beckett glared down at her and Carly wondered how she had ever thought he was handsome.

'I don't want it.'

Beckett sneered at her. 'Not now that you've snared the bigger fish.'

'Get out, Beckett,' Dare said with icy fury.

Beckett had given her the necklace! Dare could barely believe it. His senses reeled, his mind shrouded in a red haze so thick he could barely see through it.

He could feel adrenaline coursing through his system like in the old days when kids used to laugh about his loser father.

He took a deep breath and did his best to ignore the beating of his blood that wanted him to beat the crap out of his insolent cousin. If Beckett didn't leave by the door soon, he'd find himself using the window; a much quicker way to the sidewalk.

'Goodbye, my lovely Carly. It seems I'm being asked to leave.'

Beckett strolled towards Dare, a swagger in his step. He stopped and shook his head at Dare as if he felt sorry for him.

'Come in, spinner,' he said softly, laughing when Dare slammed the door in his face.

Taking a deep breath, Dare turned towards Carly. She looked beautiful and shaken standing in his living room wearing only his shirt.

He frowned. Hadn't she heard their voices? Didn't she know better than to come into a room wearing only a T-shirt?

He glanced at his well-stocked bar and wondered if it was too early in the day to have a drink.

'I never liked him,' Carly said, hugging her arms around her waist.

Dare looked at her. Why had she felt the need to tell him that? Was she feeling guilty about something? Like sleeping with his cousin right before moving on to him?

Had she lied to him?

The adrenaline hadn't left his body and he felt edgy and unsatisfied. Maybe he should have hit his cousin after all.

'Come in, spinner.'

Beckett's mocking words knocked around inside his head as if they had been shot out of a pinball machine.

Was Carly really duping him as Beckett had implied? He didn't want to believe it, but he couldn't deny the sick feeling in the pit of his stomach.

'You liked him well enough to take the necklace,' he said easily. Too easily.

'Sorry?' Carly blinked at him and then her brows drew together. 'Would you mind repeating that?'

Dare paced away from her. Maybe that hadn't

been the best thing to say given how tightly he was strung. 'I need some time to think.'

'About what?' She wet her lips as if she was nervous. But what did she have to be nervous about? *Red.* Beckett had called her Red.

Dare's teeth ground together. Had he called her that in bed? But no, Carly had claimed that she hadn't slept with him.

'Why are you looking at me like that?' she asked carefully. 'You don't actually believe there was something between me and your cousin do you?'

Dare rubbed a hand across his forehead, tried to collect his thoughts. Unfortunately they were scattered like freshly fallen leaves. 'I don't know what to believe.'

Carly stared at him. 'I already told you that Beckett gave me the necklace because he wanted me to go out with him.'

Dare stared at her. Rubbed his forehead again. 'Did my grandfather mention that he wanted us to get together?'

Carly flushed and Dare knew that he had.

'Not really.'

His eyes homed in on her like a heat-seeking missile locking onto a target. 'But he did mention it.'

'It was a joke.'

'Not one I find funny,' Dare said softly.

'You can't seriously be giving Beckett's hateful comments any credence,' Carly said incredulously. 'Dare, he was trying to get a rise out of you.'

Dare turned to her. He wasn't. He wasn't at all, but… 'What I'm struggling to understand is why a man who is in so much debt he'd throw his grandfather's company to the wolves, would then go and give a woman a necklace worth a small fortune.'

Carly felt a cold sensation slither into her stomach. 'What you mean is,' she said woodenly, 'why does a man give a woman he's *not sleeping with* a necklace worth a small fortune?'

A muscle ticked in his jaw. 'So why does he?'

Carly felt so sick she could barely breathe. 'I already explained it to you once,' she said slowly. 'He asked me out. I said no. The necklace was… I don't know…some sort of enticement, I suppose. I never asked him.'

Dare's gaze wouldn't meet hers and Carly knew then that he didn't love her. Because how could you love someone you didn't know? Someone you didn't trust?

Carly was just about at the bedroom door when Dare grabbed her arm and swung her towards him.

'Where are you going?

'I'm leaving.'

'We're having a conversation.'

'No, we're not,' she fumed. 'You're conducting an investigation.'

'I asked *one* question,' he said, as calmly as possible. 'Which apparently you don't want to answer.'

'I did answer it.' She tipped her chin up. 'Tell me you believe me.'

A heavy silence followed her request and Carly had her answer. How, she wondered, had she ever imagined she was in love with this man who was exactly like her ex?

A sob caught in her throat and she quickly stifled it.

'*Now* where are you going?' he asked irritably.

'I told you...I'm leaving. Do you need me to repeat that as well?'

Dare ran a hand through his hair. 'I just want the facts, Carly. Is that too much to ask?'

Carly clenched her teeth. 'How many times?'

'How many times what?'

'How many times do you want your precious facts until you believe them? Because once wasn't enough. Will twice do? Maybe three times. A hundred?'

Dare swore under his breath. 'Look,' he began reasonably. 'I could have made a mistake.'

Carly shook her head. This time she wouldn't be cowed by a man. 'Well, while you *could* have made a mistake, I *did.*'

Dare watched her storm into his bedroom and he headed for the balcony. He looked down at the garden below. Breathed deeply. Tried to get his head together. It didn't work; if anything he felt more confused. Was she telling the truth or was she lying because she thought it was what he wanted to hear?

When he heard his front door slam that old sick sensation from his childhood returned and he gripped the balustrade in front of him and told himself that he'd done nothing wrong.

CHAPTER ELEVEN

THAT WAS SOMETHING he was convinced of right up until he'd snatched up his helmet and straddled his bike, intending to hit the open roads. Which was when the sick feeling was replaced with a sense of hollowness.

She'd left him. She'd really walked out. And why? Because she had an unreasonable temper. No man in his right mind would want to put up with that. And what had she expected him to say after he'd seen her return Beckett's necklace? After the way Beckett had smiled at her? The way his cousin had laughed at him?

All Dare had wanted was the facts. What the hell was wrong with that? Nothing—that was what.

Except obviously there was, or he wouldn't be feeling this hollow. This empty. Nor would he be sitting on his stationary bike, breathing in petrol fumes in his underground garage.

Dare grimaced. From the moment he'd met her

Carly Evans had twisted him up and turned him inside out until he hadn't known which way was up. But not anymore. If she didn't want him then he didn't want her either. Only he did…

He shook his head. He needed to get home. Home to the Smokies. Whenever his father had gone off chasing rainbows Dare had usually spent a couple of days camping amongst the raccoons and bears. Not that he'd ever seen a bear. Much as he'd tried. Sometimes he'd been so hurt he'd wanted to fight one with nothing but his bare hands. During those times he'd felt as if he could have ripped a bear's head off.

But why couldn't he take what she said at face value? He knew the answer: people often said one thing and meant another. His father was a case in point, but there had been others. Other women who had said they loved him, but really they had loved his money and status.

But how would he know if Carly had told him the truth? The fact was a man could only really ever rely on himself. He knew that.

He shoved the helmet on his head and kicked the stand up. First he'd go for a ride to clear his head, and then he'd stop off at the hospital before heading to the office. God knew his PA didn't know what to make of all this time he was having off. Then he'd think about what to do about Carly.

Right now though, right now he was too humiliated to contemplate it. And why wouldn't he be? If their situation had been reversed, if she'd discovered a woman's earring, or say a pair of panties wedged down the side of his sofa he wouldn't mind if she gave him the third degree. In fact, he'd expect it!

Not that he'd probably see her all that often. Not once he returned to the States next week. Because all that baloney about loving her? It was called hot sex. Hot sex that had fried his brain and had him building castles in his head, not unlike his father had done with his scams.

Dare shook his head at his own gullibility. Then he pulled out his phone and punched in her number. When she didn't answer he gritted his teeth and left a message, ending with instructions to call him.

Shoving the phone back in his pocket, he roared out of the garage and headed for the hospital.

Unfortunately his mood hadn't improved much by the time he pulled up. When he didn't find a missed call from her it turned a little more grim.

He barely took any notice of the hospital staff and visitors who scrambled to get out of his way as he stalked through the hospital corridors. Then he wondered if she would be waiting for him in Benson's room, to apologise to him for being so unreasonable.

That made him smile. If you could call the twist of his lips a smile.

He paused outside his grandfather's room, took a breath and pushed open the door.

Other than his grandfather, reclining in bed watching the TV, the room was empty.

As soon as he saw him, Benson clicked off the TV.

'Dare.' The old man's eyes watered and he brusquely cleared his throat. 'It's good to see you.'

'And you,' Dare said. 'How are you?'

'As good as can be expected.'

Dare let out a slow breath ignoring the way his gut felt like it was full of rocks. 'So what do the doctors say?'

'They don't know a lot yet,' Benson said. 'The biopsy results still have to come through.'

The conversation moved on to how annoying it was sleeping in a hospital what with the nurses coming in every fifteen minutes to check his vital signs and on to the lunch menu until Dare couldn't stand it anymore.

'Have you seen Carly today? Is she with my mother?'

Benson blinked and Dare realised he'd spoken over top of him. 'Sorry. I just…I need to speak to her.'

'Your mother has gone shopping and Carly stopped by a short time ago, but now she's gone.'

'I can see that.' Dare smiled with the patience of Job. 'But where? And when will she be back? Her cell phone is switched off.' He said the last as if that explained everything. Really it only explained that she didn't want to talk to anyone. Or her battery had run flat.

'She's not coming back,' Benson said.

Dare frowned. 'But she still has a week to work out her contract.'

'Her contract was only until my operation.'

'But surely you'll need post-op care or whatever they call it?'

'Yes, but Carly is a highly trained doctor. I could hardly be lucky enough to get her to extend her services.'

'So that's it? You'll never see her again.'

'I hope not. She's a lovely young woman. I've grown fond of her.'

Dare frowned. 'How fond?'

Benson's eyebrows shot up. 'What do you mean?'

Dare shook his head. He no longer cared if his grandfather had tried to implement some Machiavellian plan to set him up with Carly. 'Never mind,' Dare said, irritated with himself. 'You were about to say something.'

'Only that I believe Carly already has a new job to go to. And speaking of work issues, I've been meaning to ask your advice about how to handle the whole Beckett situation.'

'I've got my PR people working with yours,' Dare said distractedly. 'Did you know that Beckett gave Carly a necklace?'

'What? Another one?'

Dare turned back to find his grandfather frowning. 'How many did he give her?'

'I know he gave her one with a large ruby in it.'

'That's the one I'm talking about.'

Benson shook his head. 'That boy doesn't know the value of money. What fool gives a woman a precious necklace to try and entice her to go out with him?'

Dare swallowed. 'So she never went out with him?'

Benson laughed. 'Of course not.'

Heart beating too fast, Dare saw his life flash

before his eyes. 'Many women would consider it a sizable inducement.' But even as the words left his mouth he knew that Carly wasn't one of them.

'Not a woman like Carly.'

No, Dare thought, shoving his shaking hands into his pockets, *not a woman like Carly.*

He'd been wrong. *Again.*

And suddenly his smug message replayed in his head. He was a bigger fool than he'd given himself credit for. A stupid, hard-headed fool.

He pinched the bridge of his nose. If she hadn't hated him before, she no doubt would after listening to that.

'Dare, are you quite all right?'

Dare nearly choked on his own stupidity, and knew he had no one to blame for his mistrust but himself. Beckett might have infected him with his venomous words, but Dare had made it easy for him, hadn't he? Because, as much as he'd tried to deny it, he hadn't trusted her; she'd been right about that. What she *didn't* know was that he didn't trust anyone.

'Dare, you've gone very pale.'

Dare stared at his grandfather without really seeing him. Being pale was the least of his concerns. How he was going to win back the only woman he had ever loved was much more important.

'I'm in love with Carly.'

Benson beamed. 'That's fantastic.'

'No, it's not,' Dare said tonelessly. 'I stuffed up.'

'What did you do?'

'I basically accused her of sleeping with Beckett.'

Silence fell between them.

Benson cleared his throat. 'That wouldn't have gone down very well.'

'It didn't.'

'What are you going to do about it?'

Dare looked at him bleakly. 'The hell if I know.'

'Want my advice?'

'Please.'

'Tell her how you feel. We all make mistakes, Dare. You're not perfect. And neither is she.'

Dare stared at him. 'You make it sound so simple.'

'Simple it's not,' Benson said. 'But it's a lot harder living without love. Trust me, I tried.'

Dare reached out and clasped his grandfather's shoulder. 'I'm glad you contacted my mother.'

'Best thing I did. Now go get your girl.'

Not knowing where to start, Dare did the only thing he could think of.

He called her again and told her he loved her.

He poured his heart out to her message bank and admitted that he'd been wrong and hoped she'd forgive him because she was the most important person in his life. Then he called again and told her he wanted to marry her.

By the third day when he hadn't heard from her Dare felt as if he were going mad. No one knew where she was. She hadn't been back to Rothmeyer House to collect her things, and she'd quit her job with the agency.

He'd even called her parents in Liverpool. Her polite mother had said that Carly wasn't there. When he'd called again her polite father had confirmed her polite mother's words. They hadn't seen her. And then her father had graciously advised him to never call again.

Dare stared out of his office window.

Her father, the Viking, protecting his little girl. He would have smiled if he didn't feel so, so— Dare's eyes narrowed. Why would Carly's father need to protect his daughter if he hadn't seen her?

Dare closed his eyes and when he opened them he searched the room for his helmet.

Carly glanced at her cell phone and saw another voice mail message from Dare. Without even thinking about it she deleted it. After that first message she'd had from him she'd deleted every single one since without listening to them.

What woman in her right mind would do any differently after that first pompous message about panties?

Panties?

Carly hadn't known whether to laugh or cry.

'What was that, honey?'

She glanced up from her cell phone to where her mother was making tea for them both in the family kitchen.

As it was past ten o'clock her father had bid them good-night hours ago, but, since she had arrived home three days ago, Carly and her mother had taken to staying up late into the night talking.

And it had been so cathartic to finally confront those things that had hurt her the most and face them head-on. She'd even told her parents how responsible she had felt over Liv's death and a weight of guilt had finally lifted from her heavy shoulders. Then last night she and her mother had cried themselves dry over photo album after photo album; remembering Liv, crying for Liv and loving Liv all over again.

And as for Daniel, well, she'd finally admitted

that he'd dented her pride and not her heart and that if she ever saw him in the street again she wouldn't hang her head in shame. She'd likely walk up and give him a piece of her mind.

The one person she hadn't mentioned was Dare. And it wasn't because she was trying to avoid thinking about him. It was just that her mistake over him was still too new. Too raw. Because while Daniel had only dented her pride, Dare had torn it in half, making her feel like a fool for loving him so completely so quickly.

Now she just longed for the day that she didn't wake up thinking about him. When she didn't go to bed seeing his face in her mind.

'Carly?' Her mother set tea down in front of her. 'Did you say something?'

'No,' Carly laughed reassuringly at her mother. She hadn't realised she'd spoken out loud. At the time she'd heard the message she'd replayed it twice over. She shook her head. If she had found a pair of women's underwear anywhere near his sofa she wouldn't have bothered telling him to find a high cliff, she'd have driven him to it and pushed him off it herself.

'I thought you said panties,' her mother said, setting the tea down.

'No, I said…I said…*tanties*. As in tantrums.'

Her mother made a face. 'Why would you say that?'

'I was just remembering a message I received the other day. It was nothing.'

'Was it from that man? The one with the deep voice.'

'No,' she lied.

Apparently Dare had called the house a couple of times looking for her. She'd told her parents to act nonchalant and tell him they hadn't seen her. When they had given her that worried look she'd told them he was Benson's grandson who had thought she was a gold-digger and been horrible to her.

That had been all it had taken for her father's spine to stiffen.

'Oh, well.' Her mother sipped her tea. 'He certainly has the looks to back up the voice, but what did you say he was?'

'An obstinate, hard-headed—' Carly stopped, eyeballed her mother. 'How do you know what he looks like? Did you see his picture in the paper or something?'

Her mother cupped her teacup in her hands and looked flustered. 'Not exactly.'

'On the Internet?'

'He was here.'

'In Liverpool?' Carly's heart jumped into her mouth.

'He said he was in the neighbourhood.'

'Liverpool is not his neighbourhood, Mum.'

'I'm sorry, honey. I didn't confirm you were here, if that's what you're worried about.'

Carly relaxed. Slightly.

'If he's stalking you—if he hurt you—'

Carly shook her head. 'He's not the stalking kind.'

'Then why was he here?'

'I'm sure I don't want to know.' She frowned. Checked her phone in case she'd missed a call from the Baron or Travelling Angels. She'd resigned from there as soon as she'd left London so she wasn't expecting a call but if something had happened to Benson she knew they'd inform her.

But there were no messages.

'Carly, honey, what happened with this Mr James?'

Carly felt her throat close over. When she felt she could talk again she said the first thing that came into her head. 'I was a fool.' And then she burst into tears.

'Oh, honey, I hate to see you cry.'

'I know…I'm sorry. I just…I have terrible taste in men.'

She swiped at her eyes and grabbed a tissue from the nearby box. Then she told her mother what had happened. How she had tried to resist him but he'd been…

'The kind of man to make a woman swoon?' her mother offered.

Carly grimaced. 'He took my breath away from the first moment I saw him, only he isn't the kind of man who is interested in long-term relationships and…even worse, he was the same as Daniel.'

'He cheated on you!'

'No…I meant…' Carly swallowed. 'He didn't love me either.'

'Oh, Carly.'

'It's okay.' Carly hiccupped. 'He isn't worth it.'

And one day she hoped she'd believe that. She wadded the tissue into a ball and aimed it at the kitchen sink as she and Liv had done as kids.

'Carly—' Her mother's familiar reprimand was cut short by a loud knock at the front door.

Carly glanced at her mother. 'Are you expecting anyone?'

'No.'

Her mother got up to go to the door before Carly thought to tell her to ignore it.

Then she heard Dare's voice and immediately swiped at her eyes and straightened her shoulders.

When he walked in she caught her breath. Once again he was dressed in head-to-toe black leather so she knew he'd ridden his bike up from London, but gone was the cocky charmer who had nearly run her down and in his place was a man who looked as if he'd forgotten how to shave or sleep.

A deep yearning careened around inside her chest and it took all Carly's effort not to act like Benson's ratty little dog and bound into his arms. Especially when she no doubt looked just like Gregory with her unkempt hair and her mother's thirty-year-old dressing gown over her old pyjamas. Why was it that she had a cupboard full of nice clothes but this man never caught her wearing anything *decent*?

He looked her up and down. 'You've been crying,' he said softly.

'No, I haven't. I have hay fever.'

His brows rose. 'At the end of summer?'

'All year round.' Her heart was kicking inside her chest like a racehorse trying to break out of its barrier but she'd be damned if she'd let him see her so vulnerable.

'Would you like a cup of tea, Mr James?'

'Dare doesn't drink tea, Mother,' she said stiffly.

'I didn't think you did either,' he said gruffly.

Carly wasn't about to explain that this was her and her mother's special thing. 'What are you doing here? I thought I told you not to come near me again.'

His nostrils flared at her frosty tone. 'I needed to make sure you got my messages.'

'I got the one about the panties,' Carly scoffed. 'That was enough.'

'I think I might leave you two to talk,' her mother said softly.

Carly glanced up and saw her mother's flushed face. 'Thanks, Mum.' She had been so intent on Dare she had forgotten her mother was even in the room. By the look on his face, Dare had too.

'About that message.' He tugged at the collar on his jacket. 'I wasn't exactly thinking straight when I left it.'

'You don't say.'

He ignored her sarcasm and raked a hand through his hair. 'But I was referring to my other messages.'

'I don't care about your other messages. I want you to leave.'

Dare stared at her beautiful, defiant face. Was that it? Was that all she was going to say after he'd poured his heart out to her? After the things he'd told her?

Yes, it seemed so.

He sucked in a steadying breath. 'There's nothing you want to add?'

'If I'd had something to add I would have called you, wouldn't I?'

'Of course.' Dare zipped up his jacket, swallowed heavily. 'I'm sorry I disturbed you.'

'I'm sorry I ever met you.'

She said it under her breath but Dare rounded on her. 'You know, when a man pours his heart out to you, you might want to think about being a little nicer about it.'

'Pours his heart out?' Carly gave a harsh laugh. 'That's rich,' she said thickly. 'You talk about women's underwear and demand that I call you— as if *I'm* the one at fault—and you call that pouring your heart out?'

'I never said you were at fault. If anyone is at fault I am.'

'Well, finally we agree on something,' she fumed. 'Now you can go.'

That last word came out as a sob, and Carly dashed the back of her hand against her mouth to try and contain it. Dammit, she didn't want to cry in front of him.

'Carly, I'm sorry. I didn't mean to hurt you.'

He took her face between his hands and kissed her. It was meant to be a goodbye kiss. Short and sweet. But her lips clung to his and he groaned her name and gathered her closer.

'I want you to know that I meant everything I said,' he told her gruffly. 'And if you change your mind I'll…' He took a deep breath. 'My feelings won't ever change.'

'What are you talking about?' Carly looked up at him. 'What feelings?'

Dare stared at her to the point where she became uncomfortable. Then his eyes narrowed. 'Did you even listen to my other messages?'

Carly sniffed and wiped her nose. 'One was enough.' She lifted her chin. 'I deleted the others. I didn't want to—why are you laughing?' She frowned. 'This is hardly funny.'

She tried to pull away but Dare clasped her shoulders, preventing her.

'Carly?' Dare began softly. 'Those messages you deleted.' He cleared his throat. 'They said that I love you.'

'They said…' She shrugged out of his hold and wrapped her arms around her waist. 'They said what?'

'That I love you.'

Carly shook her head. 'You can't love me—you don't trust me.'

'You're right, I didn't trust you, but I need to explain that.'

And he did. He told her about his father and how his actions had made Dare grow jaded and cynical. How he'd grown up prepared to take risks with everything other than his heart. 'With you, I couldn't seem to stop myself. Every time I tried to back off you were there, inside my head. Inside my heart.'

Carly stared at him. She wanted to believe him. She was *desperate* to believe him but something still held her back. 'What happens when another Beckett comes along? When—?'

Dare reached for her again. 'There won't be another Beckett because this time I'm giving all of myself to you just as you gave all of yourself to me the other night. Tell me it's not too late. Tell me you'll give me another chance.'

Carly looked up at him. 'But I didn't give all of myself to you,' she murmured, looking up at him. Because even though she'd thought she had, she hadn't taken the ultimate step. She hadn't told him she loved him.

'The truth is that I thought I was in love with Daniel and he used to accuse me of sleeping with other men and it was horrible.'

Dare frowned. 'You told me he had been the one to cheat.'

'He was. He did, but then he'd belittle me and I felt stupid and—'

'And I came along and did the same thing.' His arms tightened around her waist. 'I'm sorry, Carly, please forgive me. I've been a bigger fool than I first thought. That was what was on some of my other messages.' He looked down at her imploringly. 'A fool who was so afraid of getting hurt it was easier to let you walk away. It won't happen again.'

'I was afraid too,' she admitted. 'Afraid of making another mistake but I could have stayed. I could have made you listen.'

Dare shook his head. 'That wouldn't have worked because all I wanted was the facts.'

'And now?'

'And now I know that facts are well and good but they don't tell the whole story.' He leaned down and kissed her softly. 'Now I know I should have listened to what was inside my heart, not my head.'

'Oh Dare, I'm guilty of the same thing. After Liv died I felt so frozen inside by my sense of guilt and loss, at the fact that I was alive when she wasn't…even now I wish she could experience what I have right now. With you.'

'She'll always be in your heart, Red. And if you want we'll open a hospital wing in her name.'

'For kids?'

'For the whole world if you'll agree to be my wife.'

'Your wife?'

'What did you think this was? A one-night stand proposition?'

'No, I just…I thought you didn't want a long-term relationship.'

'I didn't. I didn't believe I needed love. Then you came along.'

Carly's smile was watery. 'You know, I love you so much I just want to shout it from the rooftops.'

Dare ran his hands over her arms, then cupped her face. 'Why don't you just tell me?'

'How many times?' Carly teased.

His grin was slow, but it showed that dimple she loved so much. He tugged her closer. 'Until I'm satisfied.'

'That could take a really long time.'

'It's going to take for ever, Red. For ever in my arms.'

'Yes,' Carly said, linking her arms around his neck. 'For ever sounds perfect.'

EPILOGUE

THEY WERE MARRIED the following month at Roth-meyer House, with Carly's parents and Dare's mother in attendance, along with the Baron and Gregory. Gregory got the best-man position, although Carly had already warned him that if he ran off she would not be chasing after him this time.

Mrs Carlisle cooked up a feast with tofu well and truly disguised in the mix, and Roberts was their celebrant.

Fortunately the summer days had continued into an Indian summer and the breeze was light with the perfume of late-summer blooms.

Benson's medical results had been the best anyone could have asked for and all of them hoped for many more years to make up for those that had been lost.

As for Beckett, he had apologised to both Carly and his grandfather but had yet to speak to Dare. A man had a point of pride, apparently, and fronting up to Dare and admitting he was a jerk was his.

But that was okay with Dare. He'd paid off his cousin's debt and helped BG Textiles weather the storm caused by his cousin's desperation. Because none of it mattered now that he had the one thing he'd always longed for—a family he could rely on and give his heart to.

Especially his beautiful wife-to-be who was walking towards him down the short aisle that had been laid out in the rose garden.

Both Rachel and Beth, Carly's mother, pulled out hankies, but Dare's eyes were totally focused on the gorgeous redhead in the long white sheath.

Just as she got to him Dare reached out his hand to take her from her father's arm when Gregory shot up like a rocket and started yapping for all he was worth.

'It's okay, buddy,' Dare said. 'We've got her now.'

The little dog cocked his head, yawned, and then dropped immediately at Dare's feet, his nose in his paws.

Carly shook her head, laughing. 'For all the time I've walked him and petted him he has never once done anything I've asked him to do.'

'Don't sweat it, Red,' Dare said, smoothing a

wisp of her hair back beneath her veil. 'I'll do anything you ask me to for the rest of our lives.'

Carly gazed at her husband-to-be and glanced at the large photo of Liv on a nearby stand. Yes, her sister would have adored this man and, fighting back tears, she gave Liv a small smile, silently telling her sister that she wished she were here to share in this grand occasion. Then she laid her hand in Dare's and turned to face the future with the man she loved with all her heart.

* * * * *

If you enjoyed this story,
check out these other great reads from
Michelle Conder
HIDDEN IN THE SHEIKH'S HAREM
RUSSIAN'S RUTHLESS DEMAND
PRINCE NADIR'S SECRET HEIR
THE MOST EXPENSIVE LIE OF ALL
DUTY AT WHAT COST?
Available now!

MILLS & BOON®
Large Print – January 2017

To Blackmail a Di Sione
Rachael Thomas

A Ring for Vincenzo's Heir
Jennie Lucas

Demetriou Demands His Child
Kate Hewitt

Trapped by Vialli's Vows
Chantelle Shaw

The Sheikh's Baby Scandal
Carol Marinelli

Defying the Billionaire's Command
Michelle Conder

The Secret Beneath the Veil
Dani Collins

Stepping into the Prince's World
Marion Lennox

Unveiling the Bridesmaid
Jessica Gilmore

The CEO's Surprise Family
Teresa Carpenter

The Billionaire from Her Past
Leah Ashton

MILLS & BOON®
Large Print – February 2017

The Return of the Di Sione Wife
Caitlin Crews

Baby of His Revenge
Jennie Lucas

The Spaniard's Pregnant Bride
Maisey Yates

A Cinderella for the Greek
Julia James

Married for the Tycoon's Empire
Abby Green

Indebted to Moreno
Kate Walker

A Deal with Alejandro
Maya Blake

A Mistletoe Kiss with the Boss
Susan Meier

A Countess for Christmas
Christy McKellen

Her Festive Baby Bombshell
Jennifer Faye

The Unexpected Holiday Gift
Sophie Pembroke